Guiding Elliott

Guiding Elliott

A Novel

ROBERT LEE

THE LYONS PRESS

Printed in the United States of America

Designed by Joel Friedlander Publishing Services, San Rafael, CA

10 9 8 7 6 5 4 3 2

Library of Congress Cataloging-in-Publication Data
Lee, Robert, 1947–
        Guiding Elliott / Robert Lee.
            p. cm.
        ISBN 1-55821-603-0 (cloth)
        I. Title.
PS3562.E3623G85   1997
813´.54—dc21   97-3121
                                                CIP

Dedicated to my mother
Jackie Lee
July 2, 1926–August 7, 1996
She urged me to write—taught me to laugh.

ACKNOWLEDGMENTS

I offer heartfelt thanks to all of the people who helped me through the process of writing this first novel. Thanks, especially, to Bill Kittredge, Leonard Robinson, Deirdre McNamer, Dr. Jan Willms, George McRay, and to my wife, Rosemary.

DONNIE PHILLIPS

FISHING GUIDE
BIG SKY COUNTRY

Manhattan Chapter #46
Trout Unlimited
Attn: Sydney Cross, editor

DEAR PISCATORIAL PARTNERS,

I hadn't been up to my place since October. I looked out
the window. The sun was shining—the days were getting
longer. I'd have a good two hours of fishing even after the
drive if I got my rear in gear. I moved it. I put on my
waders, grabbed my favorite fly rod—the two-piece bamboo Leonard six-weight that had been my father's—
picked up my fly vest, took two beers out of the fridge,
and was out the door.

I drank one of the beers on my way out of town and
by the time I pulled off the interstate and headed up the
gravel road, I was whistling. This was a good thing to do
even if it was my old lady's idea. I was, by God, going fishing. Damn, I still get excited. A lot of guides I know don't
fish at all when they're not with a paying client. Claim
they don't get any pleasure from it. But if you ask me,
they're in the wrong profession. Hank always laughs when
I tell him I'm going fishing. He says, "Jesus H. Christ,
Donnie, why do you always take these bus driver's holi-
days?"

But I don't need a holiday, and I never take the bus. Bus drivers don't have any idea about where a guy should go fishing and I ain't about to educate them. Hank is not a real professional guide. He is just a guy who grew up in Venice, California, moved to the wild rivers of Montana, and thought guiding might be an easy way to make a living. He has red hair like a lot of Californians, from being overexposed to the sun. He has a lot of freckles on his face, too. They are no doubt so numerous because Hank always wears his hat backwards, like he would rather be a baseball catcher than a professional fishing guide. I keep waiting for him to wise up and go home. He'll never understand why a man should fish every time he gets a day off.

Standing waist deep in a cold river waving that old Leonard is the finest way I can imagine to spend the few free hours I get. As a professional fisherman, asked to write a newsletter column for you folks caught up in twenty-four hours of rush-hour traffic, I feel obliged to offer some advice now and then. So I'll tell you the same thing I tell my fellow guides:

IF IT DON'T GIVE YOU PLEASURE, DON'T DO IT!

There was a car parked at the pull-off but I didn't pay it much mind, especially after I saw it had Washington plates. Probably just hikers. You don't see many guys out before the opener, even though it's legal if you release your fish—didn't used to see anybody, unless it was maybe

somebody you knew. So I wasn't worried: I slid that lovely
Leonard together; screwed on a reel filled with six-weight,
weight-forward, sink-tip line; threaded the line through
the guides; tied a Bitch Creek nymph onto some three-X
tippet; and headed through the woods towards my place.

You may have already guessed that I don't own my
place. Hell, the bank and I have a long-term disagreement
about my old house, which is the only piece of property
on God's green earth I guess I'll ever own. But I've thought
of this place on the river as mine ever since I found it over
twenty years ago.

There's a little uphill side trail just when you get close
enough to hear the river, and if you climb up it you'll come
to a steep cliff; from there, you can see the run before you
fish it. It is a good idea, especially if you are considering
dry-fly fishing, because you can see if there are any fish
working the surface. This early in the season I was planning to fish nymphs down deep, but I climbed the hill
anyway. I just like to look at my place.

It's a long run—thirty yards of fishable water with a
riffle at each end and lots of rocks throughout where big
fish can hide. There's an eagle that lives in this canyon,
and he often flies over my head when I'm fishing. There
are huckleberry bushes on the far side up towards the head
of the run, and a few years back I watched a mother black
bear pull those bushes down so her cub could reach the
berries. It was pretty neat even though I didn't dare walk
down to fish until the bears were gone.

But this time of year is too early for berries so I knew I wasn't looking at a bear. I just wished I was. That dark shape halfway up my favorite run had to be a man. I took my binoculars out of my fishing vest. I don't advise my clients to carry binoculars as they are just a distraction to serious fishing. But as a pro, I sometimes use them to help me read the water or look for rising fish. What I was looking at now was a client without a guide—a damned out-of-state poacher if you ask me. He was all decked out in gear from Patagonia or some other foreign country. I could see he was into a good fish, which just had to be shithouse luck, which is the kind of luck these out-of-staters always seem to have when they are trespassing on our water.

He released the trout, and he used his hemostats and didn't touch the fish, so I knew he'd been smart enough to spend money on a professional guide, at least once. I wished it had of been me, cause he sure as hell wouldn't know about this place.

I kept watching even though I didn't want to. The dude moved a couple of steps upstream just like some guide must of taught him, and he began to cast again. He wasn't much to watch with a fly rod, I can tell you that. He couldn't of reached the far bank with a rifle. But the trout must of been having a really bad day because he hooked another one on his very next cast. I couldn't stand it. I put the field glasses back in my vest and started looking around for rocks. When that rube hooked a third fish,

I began flinging them. He lucked out again. My first throw was off the mark and hit a tree because it was early in the year and my arm was rusty. And after that my shoulder began to hurt and I wasn't getting the distance. It occurred to me that, even though I just wanted to mess up his water, I was bound to hit the guy sooner or later, and with my arm so strong from rowing and casting I'd probably kill him. Which he no doubt deserved, but which would be hard to explain. So that's what saved his bacon. That, and I had to save my arm for rowing some fool client like him down the river the next day—the third Saturday in May, opening day.

He had hooked a fourth fish by the time I turned away, and it made me so damned mad I forgot to watch my step and tripped over this misplaced tree root going down the bank and slid on my belly most of the way down to the trail. My gear was spread from breakfast to Chicago. It took me a good twenty minutes to pick it all up and it was only after I had it all put away that I noticed I'd ripped a tear in my waders. You can probably imagine that I was some kinda pissed off at that poacher by then. I thought about wading out and telling him to get the hell out of my water. I should of, too, cause I hadn't gone ten steps toward my rig when I caught my fly line on a branch. I guess I should of put down the rod and walked back to undo the snarl. But by then I just wanted to get the hell out of there. So I gave a yank on that fly rod. I didn't even pull very hard; maybe the tip was weak from all the big fish I have landed with that old Leonard. I don't know. Anyway, it broke. I can fix it, but that guy sure screwed things up for me. I'll have to get up early and patch my waders before we go fishing, too. Damned out-of-staters.

I threw the rod in the back of my truck without breaking it down, which is something I never do. Then I headed for the Muddler. I have to tell you the fishing season didn't look too bright, and it hadn't even started yet. It was enough to make a man take up bowling.

I was only on my second beer when the old lady came into the Muddler. I knew she was there because every guy in the place turned around to look at her. My old lady is a looker. Of course she didn't pay any attention to those other guys, but came right over and sat down next to me. Nancy is a good three or four inches shorter than me, though she would argue about that. Her hair is a lot longer than mine, though, because she is a real woman. She has the blackest hair in America on account of there being some Spaniards in the woodpile that was gathered when her family tree fell down. I ordered a gin and tonic for her. Then I told her all about the poacher I'd found in my secret place.

She said, "Change is inevitable, Donnie."

"I know that. And I don't plan to eat none of it. I just don't want to find some bonehead from Washington fishing my favorite run, that's all."

Nancy looked at me funny then and said, "Oh, Donnie, it's gonna be a long life." She says that fairly often and

I have no idea what it means, but men were not put on this earth to understand women.

"Bob Dylan has been telling us for thirty-some years, 'The times, they are a changin',' " she said. "It just took a while for change to get to Montana."

"Well, it can just go right back to wherever those hippies like Dylan live," I said. "I don't need to change."

It graveled me some, her bringing up Bob Dylan. She has a bunch of his tapes, but we have a truce at our house. She won't play any of that hippie weirdo music when I'm home, and I won't play Merle Haggard when she's there. But you can't stay mad long when you are sitting in as fine a place as the Muddler, drinking a Pabst Blue Ribbon beer, so I just got even by singing her a few bars of "Okie from Muskogee." She sang a little Dylan back at me, and before I knew it we were laughing right out loud even though it had been such a bad day.

Then Hank, who was sitting down the bar a ways, came over. I guess he'd been listening to us because he said, "Damn, Nancy, I knew Donnie was an old fart, but I figured you were way too young for Bob Dylan."

I was gonna brain him so as he'd have one, but Nancy said it was time to leave as I had to guide the next day. She was right, and that is what saved Hank's bacon and let him live to guide another day, which was a mistake. But I'll tell you about that in the next journal entry when, once again, you'll get to go fishing with a real Montana guide.

DEAR PISCATORIAL PARTNERS,

I aimed to tell you next about how I met Elliott, but I got to thinking that you might be confused and wondering, like I did at first, just what a Piscatorial Partner is, and why I'm calling you that.

It was Elliott's idea that I become a writer: After we got back from fishing opening day he saw me reading the new message on our bulletin board at the Barbless, the note you folks from the Manhattan chapter of Trout Unlimited sent out that said, "Anglers, share your journal entries with your city cousins and we'll publish them in our monthly newsletter."

Well, I don't have any cousins in the city except for one who lives in Billings and she's a woman and we don't have much in common. So I was about to ignore your note, like I do most of the things that Wally puts on the bulletin board, when Hank and Elliott walked up and stood one on each side of me. They are both taller than me. I noticed that Elliott stands a couple of inches above Hank, who likes to claim that he's 6'1", but I may as well tell you up front that I am probably the only fishing guide you'll ever meet who never exaggerates. I am only 5'10" and more than willing to admit it. My old lady measured me against our kitchen wall once and she claims I am only 5'7", but women don't know how to measure nothing and always think men are shorter than we really are. Besides, we have an old house where all the walls are no doubt out of plumb, and no place to measure a man's height.

Anyway, I held out my elbows and didn't let these guys push me away from the bulletin board. They both read your notice. Hank snorted and said, "They're just looking for free information about where to fish so they don't have to hire a guide."

But Elliott said, "Go ahead, Number Three. Surely, you keep a journal. Send it to them. These city folks will love getting epistles from a real Montana fishing guide."

That made a lot of sense to me, once I figured out that epistles were letters about fishing. But I never have kept a journal, because I have the kind of steel-trap mind that lets me remember where I have been without writing it down. I didn't tell Elliott any of that, though. I just told him to quit calling me Number Three and to mind his own damned business. But when I got home I sat down at this typewriter and started in, so I guess you city slickers will be lucky enough to hear from a real pro, after all.

My articles to your newsletter will be your guide to everything you'll need to know for that time when you get to fulfill your life's dream and come to Montana to fish. I'll try hard not to get too technical. But I'll assume that you are all serious fishermen and not interested in anything but learning how to catch trout. If you pay attention to my fishing tips you'll know everything you'll ever want to know about fishing, except how to hold your mouth. That only comes with experience, and you'll just have to watch the facial expressions of your guide or of the successful fishermen near you, and then go home and practice in the mirror.

I started the first letter with "Dear Fellow Fishermen," but Elliott raised a ruckus over that.

"It's the nineties, for God's sake," he said. "You can't write for a gender-specific audience anymore."

"I'm not," I said. "I am writing for any gent in the audience who thinks he is man enough to brave Montana's wild rivers armed only with a fly rod."

"I mean," he said, giving me a look worse than Wally's, "that there are a lot of women who fly fish, too."

"I know that," I said. "And it's a damned shame. I was thinking about having one letter explaining to the guys that, if their wives and girlfriends want in on the fun, they should buy them a book on how to cook fish."

"You can't do that. You'd better address these letters to women, too, or you won't have near as many readers."

Well, he was starting to make some sense, but I didn't want to give up. A fisherman is a fisherman, Goddamnit, and the women can call themselves whatever they want.

But then Elliott said, "Look at it this way, Number Three. A lot of people think that hunting and fishing trips are really all about male bonding. You don't want to further that misconception, do you?"

Well, he had me there. I want every one of my readers to know right up front that I ain't never bonded with no male and I never will.

So I gave up and asked Elliott what I should call my thousands and maybe millions of readers if I can't call you fishermen. He suggested, as you can see for yourselves, "Piscatorial Partners," which is a Latin phrase, coming from the Roman Empire just before it collapsed into oblivion and people started speaking English.

I have a good vocabulary for a fishing guide but I know I ain't no Rogue Scholar, so when I come upon a new word I study on it some.

Here is what I figured out about the word "piscatorial." The Roman Empire was at its peak, see, and, being it was a highly civilized sort of civilization, nearly all the men of any intelligence had taken up the sport of fly fishing. They weren't as advanced as us, of course, and hadn't yet discovered catch-and-release fishing. Anyway, the womenfolk of Rome weren't given enough to do, and quicker than you could tie a Montana nymph the streambeds near Rome were filled with effeminate females waving fly rods around just like we're starting to see in America today, even Montana. Well, one of the local anglers and scholars who was also a retired military man remarked, upon seeing all these women fishing, "Ain't that a piss-cutter!"

The empire collapsed soon after that, and historians have misinterpreted the remark and decided that "piscator" was a Latin term meaning fisherman.

I told Elliott my theory and he said, "Number Three, I didn't know you delved into language derivation."

I didn't know it either but I told him he'd be surprised what all I dove into, and to quit calling me Number Three.

Dear Piscatorial Partners,

Now that you know who you are, I can tell you about the time I met Elliott. It was opening day of the general fishing season, the day after I saw that moron from Washington fishing my favorite run.

We always meet our clients at Trudy's Spoon River Cafe, which is located on the banks of the Lewis Spoon River, which runs right through town. (You won't find that on no map.) Trudy's is a diner with only six tables and a counter with half a dozen stools. The tables are all covered with red-and-white-checkered plastic tablecloths and each one has a black plastic ashtray and a bottle of ketchup right in the center. Seems like Trudy is always there, either cooking or waiting on tables. Lots of our clients order spinach omelettes or stuff like that, but Trudy just laughs and tells 'em they can have scrambled eggs and ham, or eggs over easy with bacon or sausage, or a stack of hotcakes, same as everybody else. They usually take the cakes and nobody ever eats all of 'em. When Hank first joined the Barbless he complained to Trudy that there wasn't any no smoking section. Trudy is a big woman and she just glared at Hank, lit a cigarette, blew a big cloud of smoke right over his head, and went off to cook his oatmeal. Hank always orders oatmeal and Trudy always brings him milk and brown sugar on the side even though he never touches either one. She makes him bring his own raisins, though. Hank is always telling the rest of us, eating our bacon and eggs, that he'll dance on our graves. But I don't see anything in a bowl of oatmeal and raisins that would make a guy want to dance.

We always sit at the table nearest the window, and we all have on long-billed yellow fishing caps with BARB-LESS printed across the front, so we're easy to spot. This day only three of us had clients. Wally was only there for breakfast and to get us started and to drive the shuttle for us, which he sometimes does to save money when things aren't busy at the shop.

Wally doesn't own the Barbless. He just runs it. The guy who owns the shop and who is our big boss has some Italian name I can't ever remember. He lives in New Jersey and hardly ever gets to Montana. Mr. Italy is a big race car driver and I guess he's won a whole passel of races and has a peck of money.

In addition to wearing the caps, which we get to keep, Wally had this bright idea of assigning us numbers, so that when the clients came in they would know who their individual guide was. So we all have a number pinned to our fishing vests, which we also wear in the restaurant. I was given number three, which is of course no ranking of fishing skills or I'd of been number one. I don't know why I got number three. Wally doesn't always have a good reason for everything he does, which is why I'm gonna quit him one of these days and start my own outfitter's business. I'm thirty-eight years old and it is high time I had my own guides working for me.

I should stop here and tell you that I always wear my neoprene chest waders to breakfast on days when I'm going fishing. It's important, and if you are taking notes to improve your own fishing you should write this down:

WEAR WADERS TO BREAKFAST.

It will remind you to always be ready to go, so you can be the first one on the river and have your raft headed downstream first. It is often the first cast of the day that catches the biggest fish, and it's important to be the lead boat so some clumsy caster doesn't put the fish down before you get a chance at them. Of course, wearing chest waders to breakfast does make it hard to pee after you've had six or eight cups of coffee waiting for clients who are always late, and sometimes I have to use some toilet paper to wipe a few drops off my waders before I go back into the restaurant, but that's a small price to pay.

As you have probably guessed by now, Elliott was my first client of the new year. He was right on time, too, the first client to show up. He walked into Trudy's carrying a fly-rod case, his vest, and a pair of hip boots, which are almost worthless out here. He spotted us and said, "My oh my, the happy hookers." Then he walked over to join us.

He looked us all over then said to me, "Ah, Number Three. I guess you're all mine, and all decked out and ready to go, too. Precisely the way I like 'em. We won't tell Mama."

The other guys all laughed to be polite to a client, but I figured it was gonna be a long day.

The other clients showed up soon. Hank got a doctor from Chicago and his twenty-year-old daughter. Larry drew two cops from Detroit. I would of traded Larry in a heartbeat. We drove out to a river near town that's named after a flower and that I'll call the Daffodil, because I promised the guys I wouldn't use the real names of any towns or rivers and would confuse the reader by saying west when I mean east and stuff like that.

The drive from Trudy's to the river with clients is what us guides call "small talk hell," and it's one of the reasons we like to fish as close to town as possible. We listen to whatever our clients want to talk about and we try to act interested, all the time hoping they will repeat their names so we can remember them. That's usually all we remember. I learned a lot about Elliott on the way to the Daffodil, though.

Elliott is a schoolteacher, hired just this year. He teaches Spanish, English, and creative writing at the high school right here in town. That probably explains how he recognized my talent and why he wanted me to address you readers in a foreign language. He's a quiet sort of guy and not much given to talking about himself, much like I am except when I'm writing. So after he quit telling me about teaching, it got almighty silent. After about ten minutes of teeth-grinding silence I couldn't stand it anymore, so I asked him if he was married. That is no doubt the second most asked question in the whole world of small talk, right after "So what brings you to Montana," and usually the client reaches for his wallet and drags out a couple of faded pictures of his wife and kids and bores us guides with family stories for the rest of the ride to the river.

Not Elliott, though. He was quiet for so long I was beginning to think he didn't know if he was married or not. I have been married for seven years and I haven't forgot for one single minute. I can tell you that straight out. Finally Elliott said, "Yeah, Number Three, I guess you could say I'm married. My wife is still in upstate New York. She and I are separated. We have irreconcilable differences."

I know about irreconcilable differences. That's the kind of differences that Nancy's parents claimed they had. They got divorced when Nance was only thirteen, and she got shuttled back and forth between her mom's house and her dad's house. When we were kids I thought she was the lucky one, because my mom died when I was six. But I don't think so anymore. When we first got married and lived in an apartment, we had to have one of her folks over for Christmas breakfast and the other over for Christmas dinner, because they refused to talk to each other.

Then, four years ago, we had a really bad year. My dad died in late October. He had a heart attack trying to drag a deer out of the woods. Dad always said, "If you need a good man for the job, do it yourself." But I wish he would of called me that day. I'd of drug that damned deer for him. Anyway, three months later, Nancy's father got killed when he rolled his pickup truck on an icy road halfway to Great Falls.

Soon after that Nancy's mother moved to Helena. She said she could move now because she knew "he" wouldn't get the house. She said to Nancy, "Now your father will be in Hell and I'll be in Helena. May we never get any closer."

Nancy just said, "Oh, Mother," and went for a long walk. When she came back, I knew she had been crying.

Irreconcilable differences are not much fun to be around. I said as much to Elliott and he said, "You don't know the half of it, Number Three."

Then he went quiet on me again and I was beginning to wish that God had never given us guides the gift of gab. I decided to change the subject, so I asked Elliott why he was hiring a guide. We don't get many clients who live right here in town.

Elliott said that, since he was new to Montana, he thought it was a good idea to pay for a guided trip one time so he could learn a bit about the area and how to fish it.

Right then I started to think Elliott was smarter than his name implied. As a matter of fact, Elliott, even though he is a New Yorker, had stumbled upon another one of those rules that you should write down in your fishing notebook:

KNOW YOUR WATER.

It is as important for a fisherman to know his water as it is for a drunk to know his liquor—maybe even more. If you don't know your water you won't catch half the fish in it and, even worse, you might get drowned.

Take the Daffodil. It's a slow-moving river that doesn't appear to hold any surprises. It doesn't even look like it holds many fish. I've been out on this river in the summer when it moves so slow you hardly ever get home before dark. But she'll fool ya. This river will lull you to sleep with her peaceful nature, and before you wake up you're in a narrow little channel with a heavy current with a big rock or, more likely, a big logjam down at the bottom of it. A guy has to be careful on the Daffodil. All the rivers out here are trickier than they look. That is no doubt why so many of 'em are named after women.

Anyway, I told Elliott all about the Daffodil, just like I just told you, and by the time I was done we were at the put-in, which is what we call the spot where we put the rafts in the river. I thought we'd be fishing in about five minutes. But I was wrong, the same way I thought I would of told you more than this by now.

I had passed the other two rigs right before we got to the turnoff so Elliott and I could have our raft in the water first. I jumped out of the truck and started to untie the raft from the trailer and told Elliott to get a move on and put on his boots and rig up his fly rod so as we could get downriver.

He started to, but then he got sidetracked looking at some flowers that I don't know the name of. It stands to reason that a river that is named after a flower will have a lot of flowers growing along its banks. But when you're going fishing is no time to be looking at flowers and animals and stuff. It's probably the worst habit that Elliott has as a fisherman, but it brings up a rule you just have to remember and what might be the most important fishing rule I'll give you:

**DON'T STOP TO SMELL THE ROSES UNLESS
YOU ARE ON A ROSE-SMELLING TRIP.**

By the time Elliott got done looking at the flowers and the mountains in the distance and the osprey that flew overhead, and saying, "My oh my, will you look at that," I had to pee. And by the time I managed that without dribbling on my waders, both the other rafts were already headed downstream.

"Well, Number Three," said Elliott. "Let's go fishing."

DEAR PISCATORIAL PARTNERS,

It is never easy to please a paying client. Your true professional guide is, of course, one hell of a fisherman, but it helps if he understands people, too. We often wind up practicing child psychology on adults.

Most new clients think they know a whole lot more about fishing than they really do. And they think their equipment is hot stuff, too. Their casting abilities is usually zero. So us guides have to spend all day rowing fifteen or twenty feet from the bank and risk scaring the fish, instead of staying thirty or forty feet out like we oughta. And all the time lying, saying things like, "Nice cast, Fred. Where did you learn to do that?"

When they do finally get a cast in there where it belongs and come up with a fish, us guides have to act a whole lot more excited than we really are, and we usually add several inches to the size of the guy's fish. "Oh God," we'll say, "it's been a long time since I've seen a fish that big. And you really knew how to play him, too."

I don't think there's any other profession that works as hard to please a client as us Montana fishing guides.

Things looked pretty bleak when Elliott pulled out an old Fenwick glass rod. At least it was a six-weight, which is adequate, but graphite is the thing to have today. So I offered Elliott one of the four rods I always carry. Us guides get a lot of free equipment for tips, and from company reps and stuff like that. I don't ever bring the old

Leonard bamboo rod to work. It is a slow-action rod, made for relaxing, not for working the bank from a boat. So I held out a nice graphite rod to Elliott. He refused me!

"No thanks, Number Three. I don't want to get spoiled. I better use what I've got."

I had him tie on a big weighted streamer that we in the profession call a Woolly Bugger, because that's what it looks like, and I set the boat up about twenty feet from the bank. I rowed easily against the current and said, "Elliott, try to cast that fly an inch or two from the bank, then let it sink and twitch it slowly towards you. This is good brown trout water."

Elliott looked over at the shore with all its snags and overhanging branches, which always scares a client, and said, "Okay, Number Three, but I'd be more comfortable if we were a little farther from the bank."

Oh God, I thought, this guy is really caught up on himself. But I didn't like him anyway, so I moved the boat out thirty-five feet from shore. That's where I like to be on the rare occasions I get to fish from a boat, but I knew this Elliott guy would be begging me to move in closer damn soon.

Well, was I ever surprised. You just don't expect a guy from New York, especially some guy with a fruitcake name like Elliott, to be able to cast a fly rod. But he could. Could he ever. He hauled back on that old glass stick and dropped that fly right next to the bank every cast, never using more than a couple of false casts either. I bet my mouth fell open. I didn't even say, "Nice cast, Elliott." It didn't seem necessary.

Elliott is a graceful caster, too, which is something I confess I'm not, though I'm a better fisherman than Elliott will ever be. It is a treat to watch somebody who is graceful at his sport. The cast with a fly rod is really two casts—one back behind you and one out in front. They should look exactly the same, with the same amount of force behind them and the same tight loop in the line before it straightens out. There should be no hesitation between the two casts. That is what keeps me from being graceful: I have a little catch between my backcast and my forward cast. Elliott doesn't, though. Watching this man cast so gracefully I got to figuring he must be a real athlete, so I said, "Elliott, you oughta talk to the principal about taking over as coach of the football team. I'll put in a good word for you if you want."

Elliott just said, "What the hell are you talking about, Number Three?"

I don't understand how a man can get himself all educated and become a teacher of something as important as children and still be so slow on the draw. But fishing guides are famous for our patience so I just explained it to him, all the while keeping him just the right distance from the bank so he could keep casting.

Our high school team, The Rainbows, have been the bottom feeders of the league for as long as anybody can remember. I figure what they need is a new coach. Old

Mr. Saben is a good guy and everything, but he teaches algebra. Teaching algebra to teenagers is about all a grown man can handle. I took algebra twice when I was in high school, and there are a lot of kids not near so smart as me. It is no wonder that Mr. Saben doesn't have time to field a winning football team. I figured Elliott would be perfect for the job.

"Face it, Elliott," I said. "Teaching English to a bunch of kids who have been speaking the language since they first opened their mouths isn't exactly what I would call a full-time job."

Elliott just said, "I don't like competitive sports, Number Three."

Can you believe that? I was thinking about throwing Elliott right out of my boat for not being a real American, and I would of, too, but right then he hooked a fish.

There are a lot of trout in the Daffodil, and if you cast the way Elliott was you're going to catch some. This was a good one. I slid the raft into some quiet water and let him play the fish, which was a nice brown trout. When he got it to the boat I netted it for him.

"Nice fish, Elliott," I said. "He's a good sixteen inches."

Elliott looked down at the fish, and then at me. "Number Three," he said, "how long is your dick?"

Well, that bothered me quite a bit, a guy with a name like Elliott asking me a question like that. I began to have my doubts about him again and I decided I was wrong about his being coaching material. But I can take care of myself so I just stared right back at him and said, "I don't know. I never measured it. About nine inches, I'd guess."

"That's what I thought," said Elliott. "Number Three, there's no way this fish is more than thirteen inches long, and if you'll wait a minute I've got a tape measure here in my vest, and I'll prove it."

But I released the fish before Elliott found his measure. I was afraid it would die if we kept messing around. Besides, it is bad to show your client up to be a liar, and that fish was a good sixteen, maybe even seventeen inches.

Elliott caught quite a few fish in the next couple of hours. He could of caught a lot more, too, but Elliott can't keep his mind on business. He'd sometimes stop fishing for five or ten minutes just staring at the mountains, while we were floating by some of the best trout water in the river. "What's the name of that mountain range, Number Three?"

"Hell, Elliott, I don't know. You'll have to look it up on the map Wally's got back in the shop. Will you fish, for Christ's sake?"

But Elliott was never in a hurry to fish. He made me stop so we could watch some deer swim across the river. And he must of taken fifty pictures, including some of a bunch of mergansers, which are ducks you can't eat and which eat fish. I'd rather shoot them with a gun than a camera.

It pains me to think what a good fisherman Elliott could be if he wasn't so easily distracted. He could probably even be a guide himself if he would just pay attention to what I'm trying to teach him. I hate to harp on the same subject over and over, but when you are fishing you have to be just fishing.

IF YOU HAVE A CAMERA, LEAVE IT AT HOME.

Your guide will have a camera and he won't be tempted to take pictures of anything but the fish you catch.

Like I said, Elliott was catching quite a few fish, but it was still gnawing on me that we were the third boat in line and that if we could get ahead of Hank and Larry, we could be catching even more fish. I had a plan, too.

You see, on this stretch of the Daffodil there is a great blue heron rookery, which is what they call a place where herons have their nests, and I know that Hank and Larry always pull their boats in there so their clients can see these birds. I think they believe it will get them a bigger tip, but I know that all a client who travels all the way out to Montana cares about is lunker trout, so I never stop at the rookery. So that's where I figured to pass Hank and Larry and show Elliott some real fishing.

Elliott wouldn't have any of it, though. As soon as he saw those big nests in those cottonwood trees nothing would do but that we stop and look, even though Hank and Larry and their clients already headed back towards their boats. Elliott even said, "Number Three, who's paying whom here?" which was a mighty ungentle-manly thing to say. I pulled the boat to shore and we lost our chance to take the lead.

Great blue herons are huge birds and they look like they come from another planet. Or if they come from this one they were here before man came along and began to tame things down the way they belong. I like birds as much as the next guy, probably even more. They are some of God's neatest inventions, especially the ones He put here to sing pretty songs for us or to protect us from mosquitoes. I like some birds almost as much as I do trout. But I never stop to gaze at great blue herons, because they are a fish-eating bird and no friend to a fishing guide who is dependent upon fish for his very survival.

Elliott had a pair of binoculars in his vest and he drug them out as soon as we got to shore. There is another rule for you:

DON'T CARRY NOTHING IN YOUR FISHING VEST THAT YOU DON'T NEED FOR FISHING.

It will just weigh you down and make it hard to find the things that you do need.

Nothing would do but that we trudge over to the rookery and lie down right underneath these cottonwoods and watch these birds. I was getting nervous; I pulled my yellow long-billed fishing hat down as far as I could and refused to look up. Great blue herons are damn big birds, and these were a long ways up in the cottonwoods. I was worried about droppings. But Elliott didn't seem worried. He just started watching them through his binoculars, all the time saying, "My oh my," the way he does.

I thought we ought to be going but Elliott handed me the binoculars and, since he was the one paying, I took a look. I'd hate to be a fish and look up through the water like I was looking up through those binoculars and see one of these critters. I can tell you that. Cottonwood trees can grow forty or fifty feet high near the river, and these birds had their nests in the top branches. It's wild to see one of these prehistoric-looking monsters come in to land on a tree branch. It's like a B-52 trying to land on a helicopter pad, only it's a B-52 that was made before they invented airplanes. I couldn't believe it. I even saw one of 'em feeding its baby pieces of a fish it had brought back from the river. It looked to be a nice brown trout, which bothered me some, but I was still pretty interested in the operation, having never seen nothing like that before. After a while Elliott said, "Ah, Number Three, don't you think we ought to go catch some fish?"

He caught a few more and we stopped at an island I know about for lunch. We were only an hour's float from the take-out so after lunch I rigged up my fly rod. Wally is death on us guides fishing when we have a client, but Elliott said he didn't mind and I thought it would do him good to watch a pro in action. This island has some really good water on both sides of it, so we waded near each other and we caught a lot of trout. At first Elliott was catching almost as many as I was, but after a while he got to poking around looking at some buttercups that were coming up through a patch of snow and I got ahead of him.

"Elliott," I said, "do you know why I catch more fish than you do?"

"No, I don't Number Three," he said. "Why do you?"

"Because I never get distracted," I said. "I think like a fish."

I thought Elliott might get offended at me, criticizing him like that. But he just laughed the way he does and said, "You know, Number Three, I was beginning to suspect that."

It made me proud. There's hope for Elliott yet. I just wish he'd quit calling me Number Three.

Dear Piscatorial Partners,

It never fails but what fishing season starts and we get in a day or two with paying clients, and then spring rains and melting snow bring the runoff and we're all left high and dry, waiting for the water to go down and clear up so we can go back to our chosen profession—guiding folks like you down our famous and ever-dangerous rivers. At least this season I am also being a professional writer, and high water gives me a chance to catch up to present tense.

Wally hung your May newsletter on the bulletin board today and, since we're just waiting for the water to clear, we all had a chance to read the good parts. The boys all teased me some about being a published writer, but I could see they were all proud and a little jealous. Especially Hank. He said, "Jesus H. Christ, Donnie! Why don't you just draw them a map?"

But I already explained to you why I ain't drawing no maps and why I'm keeping so many things secret. If Hank wants all his California friends and everybody from big states like Ohio and New York out here, he will have to draw his own maps. Then it will be on his head when our streams are all catching on fire.

I was a little put out that you only printed five pages out of all I sent you and them not in order. You print kinda small, too, but I guess most fishermen interested in fishing a tough state like Montana would be young guys with good eyes.

Elliott has been hanging around the shop most days after school. I guess he doesn't have many friends, being he is so new to town. He said you had to edit my work or it would take up your whole newsletter. "You do run off at the mouth a bit, Number Three," he said. "And you have a tendency to deviate from your subject."

Well, I almost busted him for that. I ain't no deviate and I don't write any words that won't help a boy become a good fisherman.

I read most of the article you called "The New Manhattan Project," which I thought was too long but was all about cleaning up the rivers in New York State. I wish you luck, but it probably can't be done. I told Elliott that the first Manhattan Project must of been an awful bust if you thought you had to do it all over again.

I'll write to you some more but I think you ought to consider printing everything I say and not include so many articles about fishing in Belize or Bermuda or wherever. No doubt those places don't have any trout in them, and aren't worth the trip.

Dear Piscatorial Partners,

The runoff is settling down; rumor has it that the salmon flies are out at Stony Creek, and Wally just called to say he has clients for Hank and Larry and me tomorrow.

Hank and I have a bet going—a hundred bucks says my clients catch more trout than his do. He'll probably have them using his favorite fly, the Golden Stone, so it will be like taking money from a baby as I have tied up two boxes full of number four Bullet-Headed Salmon Flies.

Elliott will drive the shuttle. I guess Wally figured that if Elliott was gonna keep hanging around the shop, he may as well put him to work. It's too bad Elliott can't float Stony Creek with us, as it is high and rolly and not for the timid. I'll give him a few flies so he can fish while he waits for us.

Hi again,

I did not use the formal greeting because I'm writing this in the evening of the same day. I was just over at the Muddler having a beer when it occurred to me that there is some things you need to know before we go fish the salmon fly hatch on Stony Creek.

Stony Creek is what they call a blue ribbon trout stream on account of it being fished once by a rich New Yorker during the salmon fly hatch. Well, after he got done being scared of those big bugs crawling up and down his neck and arms and inside his glasses like they will, he put one on a hook because he was, of course, a bait fisherman. He caught more trout in one day than there probably is in the whole state of New York. Naturally, he wanted to come back and bring a whole passel of his friends. But being a city slicker all the mountains and streams looked the same to him, and he was afraid he couldn't find Stony Creek again. So he tied a blue ribbon like the kind your wife wins at the fair for her apricot preserves to a tree near where Stony Creek runs into the Lewis Spoon River.

What he should of tied a ribbon on was the salmon fly. He caught so many fish because The Hatch was on. Here in Montana we have a lot of insects and a lot of hatches, like mayfly hatches and caddis fly hatches and the like. But there ain't nothing like the salmon fly and when we talk about The Hatch, we are talking about the salmon fly hatch.

Since I have become a professional writer as well as a fishing guide I have been reading a lot of books by the competition. As you no doubt expected I haven't learned nothing new about fishing, and not very much about writing neither. But I did notice that most of 'em do have a section on the salmon fly.

Most fishing books have a drawing or a photo of the salmon fly right on the front page of the chapter, and a lot of 'em have that picture right on the cover of the book, too. You won't see any of that nonsense here. If I can't describe a salmon fly in words I don't deserve to be calling myself no writer. Besides, I don't have a camera, even though I already told you that most guides do. I was going to buy one two years ago, but the water pump went out in my truck before I got to Kmart.

Cameras are cheating, anyway. A book about the art of fly fishing should only contain real art, which pictures out of a camera ain't. Mr. Kodak and Mr. Nikon might be smart guys but neither one of 'em is a true artist like Charlie Russell or Mary Ellen Hopkins.

Now, that lady can draw. And she looks damn good in a bikini, too. I even thought of asking Mary Ellen if she would draw a salmon fly for your newsletter, but I was afraid the old lady would pitch a fit even though the arrangement would be strictly professional. I think Mary Ellen has a boyfriend anyway, or maybe she's weird or something. A lot of them artists are, you know. She doesn't wave to me when I drive the truck by her house and blow the horn at her, so I know she must have a boyfriend or a girlfriend or something.

I'd of drawn the damn bug myself if my father hadn't stifled me at an early age. I was gonna take piano lessons in the seventh grade when I found out that Suzy Jenkins played the piano. But my father said the piano was for sissies—said one Liberace in this world was one too many. "Besides," he said, "just look at your hands. You can't play the piano with those short stubby fingers."

So I looked, and after that I give up on the piano. And that's why I took shop class instead of art, even though Billy Clark's sister, Carla, was in art class and was sweet on me. Eddie Taylor told me he got Carla's bra off at the drive-in movie. But I looked at my stubby fingers and decided to take shop, where I made a napkin holder that looks like a dog. And Carla married Andrew Brown who works at the bank and never will amount to a hill of ants.

I never did learn to draw or play the piano. Only now I make most of my living tying flies and I know my fingers ain't short or stubby. So it was all on account of my father that I wasn't no child prodigious. And he's the real reason there ain't no picture, here, of a salmon fly.

They named the salmon fly wrong. First off, it is not a fly you use to catch salmon, the way a trout fly is a fly you use to catch trout. Flies to catch salmon are big gaudy saltwater flies with fancy names like Silver Doctor or Lady

Godiva. I can tie that kind of salmon fly and if you're planning a trip to the West Coast or Alaska to fish for salmon, write to me c/o the Barbless and I'll send you six or eight dozen. But they are a pain in the ass to tie, and I'll tell you right up front they ain't cheap.

The salmon fly that hatches around here is not so named because salmon eat them, either, though I'm sure they would if there was any salmon around here. But there ain't, thanks to the Army Corps of Engineers, which descended on the West and dammed all our rivers because there weren't enough wars.

The salmon fly was named on account of its color. They named it wrong.

The body of the salmon fly is orange, but as you know the outside of a salmon is silver—unless you buy one in a grocery store in Montana. Then it has probably turned a sort of greasy gray. The flesh of a salmon is orange and that is supposedly how the salmon fly got its name, but that's silly, too, since salmon flies are native to Montana and salmon are native to the coast, and by the time a salmon gets here by truck and laid out on ice in a store to be sold at four-something a pound, its flesh has turned brown.

So if they were being accurate they would of named the salmon fly the "fresh-salmon-flesh-colored trout fly," which is too much of a mouthful even for a German brown trout, which will eat mice and baby ducks and would probably eat a hot dog with sauerkraut if you could tie the pattern.

The salmon fly should be named the robin fly. The body of a salmon fly is almost exactly the same color as the feathers on a robin's breast. In fact, I have a good wet-fly pattern that uses those feathers, but I don't dare tie it. The robin is protected by law, just like the spotted owl. Fish-eating ospreys and eagles are protected, too. And so is the raven and even the damn magpie, which is such a cocky bird I can hardly keep from killing every one I see. We have too many laws protecting everybody but fishing guides, and that is because there are so many vegetarians and even a few lesbians in Congress.

I'll finish this article on the salmon fly by offering up another rule for you to put in your notebook:

**DON'T BE DISTRACTED FROM YOUR
FISHING BY WATCHING THE HATCHING,
WEIRD STUNT FLYING, OR MATING
OF THE SALMON FLY.**

The salmon fly is one of God's strangest creatures. It lives under stones in the water for two years (which is why it's also called a stone fly) and then crawls up on a willow branch, cuts a hole in its own shell, and flies out over the stream looking for a few hours of fun and sex, and usually gets eaten by a trout or a robin before it has much of either. I have spent hours watching them myself, but that is for after you're done fishing and you're having a cold Pabst Blue Ribbon or a hard-earned mouthful of whiskey.

DEAR PISCATORIAL PARTNERS,

My dad always used to say, "This too shall pass," but he never worked for the likes of Wally.

I was just a bit late getting over to Trudy's this morning. To be honest, I missed breakfast altogether, which is the only reason I can think of why Wally treated me the way he did.

When I got there the place was plumb full of clients and guides, but I was the only one wearing waders, which will show you that if you follow the rules in these articles you'll be way ahead of everybody else. Anyway, when I walked in I heard some woman say, "Well, I'll be dipped, that must be Number Three."

Then Wally, who has been my friend for a hundred years, hollers out, "Hey Number Three, come over here and meet your client."

I couldn't believe my ears. Not only did Wally, who knows I'm his best guide, call me Number Three in front of everybody else, he said "client." It couldn't be true that on Salmon Fly Day, when every damn guide in town was working Stony Creek, I'd end up with only one client, an unbalanced boat to wrestle down the creek, and half the tips. I gave Wally a look even he would of been proud of and headed over to meet the lucky guy who would have me all to himself. Halfway there I saw that Wally wasn't with no guy except Elliott, of course, who was standing next to him and my client, the "I'll be dipped" woman.

I thought right then about quitting the business and I would of, too, if the old lady hadn't just gone shopping yesterday and bought enough food to keep us in the poorhouse for a month. The woman has no self-control. I went on over.

My client's name was Beth. She's a lawyer. That surprised me. She's a redhead but is from Burlington, Vermont, and does not have many freckles on her face. She's pretty if you like skinny women, but she has a sharp nose like a lot of lawyers do from rubbing up against other people's business. She's a good two inches taller than me even though she is a woman. There is no accounting for God's decisions, sometimes, but I wouldn't want His job. I'd guess Beth to be about thirty, but she must be one of those women who jog all the time in tight yellow leotards so men will look at them, because she's in damn good shape. She didn't do much for me, but Elliott looked like a bird dog ten steps from a pheasant. The first thing Beth said to me was, "I like your waders."

I felt better. At least the woman knew quality when she saw it. My waders are the new neoprenes with the boot made right on them so you don't need wading shoes. They are the best money can buy. Of course, I didn't buy them. A client gave them to me for a tip last year. They're a half size too big but that doesn't matter. I started to describe them to her, but a woman doesn't have much of an attention span. She started to roll her eyes at Elliott, who rolled his back.

Wally told me he was going to run the shuttle and let Elliott go along with me to get the feel of some real water. He said he was thinking about having Elliott row the supply boat next week when we would float the Jones River, which I'll talk about later and which you won't find on no map.

I understood then why Wally was leaving his best guide with only one client. It was a training trip for Elliott. That was all well and good, but it wouldn't put any extra money in my pocket. I wondered why Wally was getting so damned chummy with Elliott. And I was still sore about Wally calling me Number Three. I don't know how I'm gonna get rid of that damned handle now. To make matters worse, Hank wouldn't let me out of the bet.

"You've got two rods in the boat, same as me," he said. "You aren't going to welsh on a bet, are you, Number Three?"

It made me mad, him calling me Number Three and hinting that I was Welsh when he knows I'm one hundred percent Montanan. But Elliott said, "Don't worry, Number Three. We'll whip 'em. I'll think like a fish all day, I promise." He laughed like he does, and that damned Beth rolled her green eyes at him again.

"What the hell," I said. "Let's go fishing."

Dear Piscatorial Partners,

**DON'T NEVER GIVE UP ON A DAY,
EVEN IF YOU ARE CASTING BAD OR IT'S
RAINING OR THE WIND IS BLOWING OR
YOU MISSED BREAKFAST, OR THERE IS A
WOMAN IN YOUR BOAT.**

Beth surprised me at the put-in by saying, "Elliott, get the lead out. We won't catch any fish with you standing around staring at the scenery."

Elliott did, too, and our raft was in the water a good five minutes ahead of Hank's, which would give me all the advantage I'd need if I didn't have a woman client. It pained me to give Beth the front seat in the raft and to stick Elliott, who was my only hope against Hank, in the back where the fishing is harder. But Beth was the paying client and Elliott wouldn't take the front seat, even after I explained to him in a whisper that Beth probably wouldn't even know the difference.

Elliott probably saved my bacon on that one. This woman had been fishing before. She took out a seven-weight graphite rod that had to cost three hundred dollars and I said, "See that, Elliott? Beth has better equipment than you do."

"She sure does," agreed Elliott, grinning like it didn't matter. Beth said, "Oh, for Christ's sake, let's catch some fish," so I handed her a Bullet-Headed Salmon Fly, which she tied on without asking for no help. I put a box of those flies where she could reach them, handed Elliott the other box, and we headed downriver.

The Stony was running bank full but it was clear, and there were a lot of salmon flies in the air already even though the sun hadn't been on the water long. I figured we'd catch some fish if this woman could cast at all, but I knew I couldn't pay much attention to her because rowing the Stony at high water is a full-time job and not for the faint hearted. I made sure we were all wearing life jackets.

WEARING A LIFE JACKET DOES NOT MEAN THAT YOU ARE UNDER TWELVE YEARS OLD.

And if you're over twelve, there's no one big enough to make you wear a life jacket if you don't want to. But you can, and that is my point. You no doubt still follow a lot of the rules your mama taught you even though you're all grown up—like, "Don't pick your nose in public." Well, not wearing a life jacket on the Stony during runoff can be just as embarrassing as being caught with a booger on the end of your pinkie.

Don't get me wrong. I can swim, and I don't wear my life vest all the time, like when I'm floating the Daffodil in midsummer. But the Stony is nothing to be sneezed at in the last week of May. So I had my hands full just rowing, but I could see that Beth could handle a fly rod a lot better than I had expected. She was chucking that Salmon Fly right in against the willows just like she should. I was proud of her. But the damn fish weren't cooperating. I saw several roll up and look at her fly, but she must of been doing something wrong, for they wouldn't take it. Elliott wasn't having any better luck, and I could picture myself handing Hank a hundred dollars and then having to give the old lady hell for buying so many groceries.

But Elliott finally hooked and landed a nice fish. I said it went fifteen inches but Beth rolled her eyes and I worried what she might say. You don't never know what's gonna come out of the mouth of a woman what's all mixed up in her jeans and has become a lawyer. But she just said she'd heard that line before and this fish wasn't any more than eleven inches long. I didn't argue with her. I could see she was jealous that Elliott was catching all the fish.

He caught another one right away, then a third. "Okay, Goddamnit," said Beth. "Give me one of those hot flies."

"It's the same as yours," I said, but Elliott reached over my shoulder and handed her a box of Royal Wulffs.

"I changed back there a ways, Number Three," he said. "They seem to like this baby more than that big bug today."

I couldn't believe it. Beth clipped off the Salmon Fly and began to tie on a Royal Wulff. "I'd stick with the real McCoy if it was me," I said, but Beth just raised one eyebrow, tied on the Wulff, and caught a sixteen-inch brown on her first cast.

Still, I'll say to you, and you should write it down:

FORTY-SEVEN TIMES OUT OF FIFTY YOU WILL CATCH MORE FISH BY MATCHING THE HATCH THAN YOU WILL WITH AN ATTRACTOR PATTERN.

This was just one of those weird days, though. In the next two hours Beth and Elliott caught a whole passel of fish—forty-two according to Beth, who was the official counter for our boat. I won't argue with her, her being a lawyer and a paying client and all, but I figured closer to sixty. Beth and Elliott were having a good time, too, whooping and hollering when they caught a fish, holding up some puny little trout and saying things to me like, "What do you think, Number Three?—twenty inches?" I'd just nod and say, "Nice fish, Fred," even if it was Beth holding up the trout.

It usually was, too. Elliott fished hard at first and I really think that he was trying to think like a trout, but he just doesn't have what it takes. Before long he was counting deer, and making me pull over so we could all see a moose he spotted. I was some put out as it is hard enough just to row the Stony in May without having to pull over to a stop to look at what must of been one of God's early attempts at a cow. Once you have seen one moose, you have seen the whole show. But when I pointed this out to Elliott, both he and Beth said that this was their first, and to leave it be. Beth even said, "Who's paying whom here, Number Three?" which made me think that Elliott had been telling tales out of school while I had been missing my breakfast.

I didn't even wait for them to ask, twenty minutes later, when we spotted the bear. I just pulled over to the far bank and handed Elliott the dry bag so he could dig out his camera and binoculars. I have to tell you that I probably would of pulled over to watch the bear even if I'd been alone.

IT'S OKAY TO STOP FISHING FOR FIVE MINUTES TO WATCH A BLACK BEAR, AS THEY ARE A RARE CREATURE AND ONE OF GOD'S EARLY ATTEMPTS AT MAKING A MAN, WHICH NEARLY SUCCEEDED. TEN MINUTES ARE OKAY FOR A GRIZZLY BEAR, BUT MAKE SURE YOU ARE ON THE OTHER SIDE OF THE RIVER.

This bear must of been retarded, because it was eating dandelions. The old lady tried to feed me dandelion greens last spring, but I told her I was a good provider and she could buy beef and potatoes at the store as long as she didn't go crazy. We needn't be eating any weeds in the Donnie Phillips household. This bear, though, looked like he was having a regular feast, and I had to laugh watching him through Elliott's binoculars. Finally Beth asked me if maybe she could have a look, since this was the first bear she had ever seen. I gave her the glasses without waiting for her to remind me who was paying.

Suddenly there was a lot of hollering and the bear snorted and ran off through the willows. Hank's boat came by and both his clients were into a fish. "Hey, Number Three," Hank hollered. "How's the picture taking? I hope you brought your wallet."

Then they were out of sight. The bear was gone, but I could still picture him eating those damn yellow flowers. Hank might win the bet but it didn't seem to matter so much anymore. It didn't even bother me that Hank's boat was in the lead. "What the hell," I said, "as long as we're stopped, we might just as well have some lunch."

We did, and while we were having a sandwich and a beer I gave Elliott a little more information about fishing. "You know, Elliott, that Royal Wulff is working damn well today, but it usually won't. It's an attractor pattern and doesn't imitate anything that you'll find in nature. It is red-and-white fluff, and I call it the strawberry shortcake fly."

Elliott didn't get the point, which probably doesn't surprise you any more than it did me. "Hell, Number Three, why would a trout want a big old slimy bug for breakfast when it can have strawberry shortcake?"

Before I could answer, Beth chimed in with, "Eat dessert first, for life is uncertain."

Elliott looked at her and said, "I have that saying hanging in my kitchen."

Beth smiled and said, "I have it in my bedroom."

They rolled their eyes at each other. "Let's go fishing," I said.

Then Beth really surprised me. She said, "Number Three, let me row for a while. You can fish."

I laughed and said, "You must be kidding, Beth. This is no millpond, you know. There's rocks in this river that will eat your lunch."

"Come on, Number Three," she said, "I can handle it. Besides, you'll get to fish, and that'll give you a better chance to win that hundred from Hank."

That made some sense, but letting a client row the boat is against all the rules of guiding and I am sure Wally would fire me, if he found out.

THE PERSON AT THE OARS IS THE CAPTAIN OF A RIVERBOAT AND IS IN CHARGE OF THE WHOLE SHOOTING MATCH. DON'T GIVE THIS RESPONSIBILITY TO NO WOMAN OR OTHER PERSON WHO CAN'T HANDLE THE PRESSURE.

It's a good rule, and I don't really know why I broke it. I guess I really did want to take that hundred off Hank. After arguing a little more I let Beth row, and I got in the front seat. Elliott offered me a Royal Wulff but I tied on a Bullet-Headed Salmon Fly. "Now I'll show you how to catch the big ones," I said.

But I was nervous at first with Beth rowing so I missed a strike, cause I was too busy looking downstream.

"Relax, Number Three," said Beth, "I know how to handle this river." Then she said something in a way that I had never heard before. It tells you in one sentence how to get your bacon out of a pickle. This rule is a quote from a woman lawyer but still should be underlined in your angler's notebook:

"FACE YOUR DANGER AND ROW YOUR ASS AWAY FROM IT!"

That is really all you need to know about rowing a boat. Beth was doing a damn good job of it, too, and I had no real reason to be nervous but I must of been, because I couldn't buy a fish. Those trout kept coming up to look at the Salmon Fly but they wouldn't take it. Meanwhile Elliott caught three or four more fish and kept offering me a Royal Wulff. I wouldn't take one, though. A man has his pride.

I don't know what happened next; Beth must of taken a wave wrong or something, because my cast got away from me and I ended up hooking myself in the back of my fishing vest. Beth laughed and clipped the fly off my line. "You may as well try a Wulff now," she said.

So I did. Hell, she was the one who was paying. I started catching fish, too. We must of just gotten into some better water. I am sure that the Salmon Fly would of worked even better. Anyway, I know that Elliott and I caught twenty or thirty fish in the next hour, but Beth, who was paying and who was our official counter, said it was nine and our total for the day was fifty-one.

Beth caught two more after I started rowing again. That made our total fifty-three. At the take-out, Hank's official counter said their boat accounted for fifty-two fish. I was a hundred dollars richer and Hank was mad as hell. I had a nervous moment when Hank came over to my boat and checked the flies that Beth and Elliott were using. But they had both tied on a number four Bullet-Headed Salmon Fly, which I still say is the best damn fly there is for fishing The Hatch.

DEAR PISCATORIAL PARTNERS,

This article will be about the manly art of killing so if you are squeamish, don't read it just before bedtime.

You are probably all shaking your heads in wonder when you hear me talking about catching over fifty fish in a day, and it occurs to me that you might have a picture in your mind of a boat almost full of dead fish, and of my old lady cleaning fish half the night at the kitchen sink and then smoking and canning trout all the next day. But that's not how we do it out here, and I want to talk to you now about catch-and-release fishing.

When I told Elliott I wanted to write a letter informing you about the importance of catch-and-release fishing, he told me not to get up on no soapbox.

"It's easy for new writers to fall into the trap of hearing their own voices," he said. "I'd hate to see you start pontificating, Number Three."

I said I didn't have no soapbox to climb up on and I'd like to know whose voice I was supposed to be listening to if it wasn't my own. As for pontificating, I told him not to worry his head about anything like that.

"Hell, Elliott," I said, "I bet there will be a lot of young boys reading my letters, and you don't have to worry about me putting no thoughts like that in their heads. I want them to concentrate on fishing."

IF ALL YOUNG MEN CONCENTRATED ON FISHING INSTEAD OF ANYTHING ELSE

UNTIL THEY WERE AT LEAST, SAY,
THIRTY YEARS OLD, THIS OLD WORLD
WOULD BE A BETTER PLACE.

I should tell you right up front that I have killed a lot of fish in my life. When I was growing up I never heard of such a thing as catch-and-release fishing. Our freezer was always full of trout and we had a smoker, too. We mostly smoked whitefish, and Dad even pickled some. But we also killed and ate a lot of trout, and this is where Hank and I have serious trouble.

Everybody knows there ain't nothing growing wild in California but vegetables, so, naturally, Hank is a vegetarian. He never did eat meat, not even fish or chicken. Chicken is the tofu of the animal kingdom but Hank won't even eat that. So every once in a while he gets off on his high horse and starts going on about how it is guys like me and my dad, with our smokers and our freezers and our, what he likes to call, "meat-eater mentality" that has come close to ruining the fishing in Montana.

That gets me going in a hurry, I can tell you. It's just as plain as the fact that my nose has been broke twice (both times over at the Muddler, and both times sucker punches) that, before Hank and all these out-of-staters started coming to Montana, there was plenty of fish to go around. Why, Dad and I used to eat trout bigger than the "trophy fish" hanging on the walls down at the Barbless. Hank says that proves his point exactly, but I'll be damned if he's got a point.

One day when we were having this argument for about the millionth time, Elliott was listening.

"You have to admit, Number Three," he said, "that part of the responsibility for having all us out-of-staters in Montana rests with you and everybody in your profession."

Well, I sure as hell didn't have to admit to any such thing and I told ol' Elliott that in short order. "Just who the hell do you think you are?" I said. "And who asked you, anyway? Just whose side are you on? I thought we were friends, and I sure as hell never invited any out-of-staters to come catch my fish, and buy up all the land, and put up no trespassing signs, and pollute everything."

"But you'll take their money," Elliott said, "and your boss advertises in *The New Yorker* and *The Wall Street Journal,* among other places."

"Jesus jumped-up Christ, Elliott," I said. "You just don't know what you're talking about. My taking money from these people has nothing to do with it, because they are already here and bound and determined to go fishing; somebody's gonna take their money. At least I am a true professional and give them their money's worth. Besides, you must be the only fisherman in the whole world what reads *The Wall Street Journal,* so Mr. Italy is whistling in the dark."

Well, Elliott didn't have nothing to say to me after that, and Hank started looking smug, thinking he'd won the argument. So Elliott said to him, "But Hank, I think your values are all mixed up. I don't think you care a damn about the fish. You only want to catch the same trout again tomorrow so you can collect another big tip."

Then Elliott walked out of the shop before Hank could get anything to come out of his mouth, even though it was hanging open like a dog panting by the fire. That's something Elliott will do—leave right in the middle of an argument, and it would no doubt piss off the Pope if he was standing here in the Barbless, which he might someday since he probably reads *The Wall Street Journal* and knows all about the importance of fish to mankind. I even found myself ready to defend poor old Hank when Elliott turned and walked out the door like that.

But they both missed the point. The point is that we use barbless hooks today, and we try our best to land a fish as quick as we can and not tire him out, so we can release him in good condition and maybe catch him again tomorrow. That is all fine, but fishing started as a serious business that involved the killing of fish for meat, and we shouldn't forget it.

I want you to write down this rule and remember it. Actually, if you follow it, you won't never forget it:

**IF YOU AIN'T NEVER KILLED SOMETHING
AND TOOK IT HOME TO EAT,
YOU OUGHT TO DO IT.**

You'll learn something you can only guess at now. I think I'd like old Hank a lot more if he'd only just once kill something and own up to it.

DEAR PISCATORIAL PARTNERS,

I shouldn't even be writing to you right now, it being the middle of the day during the middle of the salmon fly hatch on Stony Creek. I should be guiding some lucky fishermen down the river. Instead my so-called friend Elliott is rowing my raft.

I ducked into the Barbless early this morning. I knew Wally would be there and I wanted to talk to him about calling me Number Three in front of the other guys, and about giving Larry and Hank two clients and just giving me one. I was sure he'd make it right by me.

Elliott was already in the shop. Wally was showing him a book that is fair at telling you how to row a raft, though I wouldn't buy this book then jump in a raft on the Stony or any of our other powerful western rivers and figure I knew all I needed to know about river floating— not by a long shot I wouldn't. Anyway, Wally was talking to Elliott about one of the pictures in this book when I walked in.

"Number Three," Wally said, like it was my God-given name, "I was hoping you'd come in early. Come on into my office. I want to talk to you."

Wally has a real small office in a back corner of the Barbless where he sometimes talks to salesmen, or calls us in to discuss a client he figures is scared of water or can't cast at all. He don't use the office very much, though, and

I had a bad feeling that maybe he heard about me letting Beth row the boat yesterday. It was worse.

"Number Three," he said, "I'm gonna give you the rest of the week off. We had a group out of Oregon cancel at the last minute so I only need Hank and Larry. That lawyer lady wants to go again, but I decided to take her myself so I could let Elliott row a bit to make sure he can handle the Jones next week. I won't need you until next Monday, unless you need a few bucks and want to drive the shuttle."

"Hell no, I don't want to drive the shuttle. I ain't no schoolboy, wet behind the ears. I'm a fishing guide. Let Hank drive the shuttle. He's just a transplanted California vegetarian. I oughta be guiding ahead of him any day."

"Hank's a good guide," said Wally, "and these two clients are from California. He speaks their language."

"Speaks their language! For Christ's sake, Wally, California is part of America. They speak English there, too. Besides, these guys didn't come up here to talk. They came up here to catch fish and I'm the guy to show 'em how to do that."

"I'm sorry, Number Three, but I've made up my mind."

Well, you can't never say that Donnie Phillips doesn't know when a conversation is over. I just glared at Wally, then I turned around and left the office. I slammed the door good and hard on my way out, too.

Elliott looked up and said, "Hey Number Three, today I'm gonna get my feet wet as an oarsman."

I told him he'd be lucky not to get his Goddamned hat wet and to quit calling me Number Three. Then I left the shop.

DEAR PARTNERS,

I have dropped Piscatorial from the greeting today because we're still not fishing. I did not go over to the shop this morning at all, or over to Trudy's either, so I don't know if Elliott drowned the whole bunch of 'em yesterday or not. I guess that I don't really hope that he did. As for that damn Hank, I hope he chokes on a cauliflower.

Nance said Wally is the one I should be pissed at (her words). "That damned two-faced old walrus is the one you should be pissed at," she said. "He's not treating you right."

I almost laughed. We used to call Wally "the Walrus" in high school because even then he had sort of a fat face, with jet black hair and heavy black eyebrows. His senior year he grew a little mustache, which he still has. Nance even dated him for a while back then; this is not a very big town. But I won her over, and probably Wally is still sore about it. I bet that's why he's treating me like dirt.

I pointed out to Nance that it doesn't ever do a guy much good to get mad at the boss unless he has just won the lottery or been offered a job guiding in Alaska. I told her that I was sorry I wasn't working this week, that she would have to go easy on the grocery shopping, and that I would eat about anything short of dandelions. Nance surprised me then. She had been getting ready for work, but she went to the phone and called her boss and said she needed half a day off for personal business. Nance has a college degree in psychology and sociology, and she works for a local home where they help people who are really messed up. They call the people they work with clients, too, and sometimes on warm summer days when the Daffodil is flowing about zero miles per hour I take some of those folks on a short float down the river for free. Only one or two of 'em has ever caught a fish but it's usually a fun day, because some of these people are laughing all the time.

Some of you no doubt think it's plumb awful that I let my old lady work, but she says she has to chase her dreams the same way I have to chase trout, and that makes sense to me. Live and let live ain't a bad saying.

Anyway, Nance hung up the phone, smiled, and said she was glad I had the day off. She took my hand and took me into the bedroom, which is okay, you know, since we have been married for seven years. She told me that if I described what went on in there, hell would freeze before it happened again. So you're just going to have to let your imaginations run wild with you. I'll say this:

IF YOU LAND THE RIGHT OLD LADY
YOU WILL FIND MORE SURPRISES AT HOME
THAN YOU WILL EVER FIND ON A
TROUT STREAM.

DEAR PISCATORIAL PARTNERS,

The rest of the week didn't go by as slow as I thought it would. I got some chores done around the house and did some whittling. And I tied a bunch of flies to use on the Jones. It's June and the Jones float starts out over five thousand feet up in the mountains, so you don't ever know what the weather will be or if you'll be needing big nymphs or dry flies, so I tied quite a few patterns.

You can't stay mad for long when you are planning a trip down the Jones River. We only make one trip down the Jones a season, and we take four days to do it. The river runs down one of those canyons God made just for man to look at, and He filled it with all manner of animals, including a fair number of rattlesnakes to keep out the meek what might have big notions about inheriting the place. The Jones runs right down the middle of the canyon the way rivers do, though you'd think it might get lost once in a while because that canyon has so many bends in it. An oarsman has to pay close attention not to get washed right up against a stone cliff, and I'm a little worried about Elliott, even though he won't have other people in his boat, only supplies. I don't know why I worry about that tall drink of water, though, after the way he has snuck in on Wally's good side and poisoned him against me.

Oh well, the trip will be fun anyway. We camp out by the river, eat good, and drink a few beers in the evening.

The fishing can be fantastic, too, if the weather gives us a break. I'm going over to the Barbless this afternoon, it being Sunday, to meet my clients.

DEAR PARTNERS,

Never have I had such a fishing season as this, and if I never have another it'll be too soon. As you can see from the greeting, we still are not fishing. It's Sunday night and this will be short because we will be heading for the Jones bright and early in the morning, though it will probably not be a bright morning at all.

I am just about through with Wally. As you know, I've been getting the bottom feeders of the client world all season, starting with Elliott. Tonight it reached an all-time low. If the old lady wasn't dependent on me I would leave Wally high and dry on the raging waters of the Jones River without his best guide.

I went to the Barbless tonight expecting to get the same two doctors who I guided last year. The Jones is not a cheap trip, and it's so wonderful that those of you who were born to be doctors or lawyers or such will be the only ones besides us fishing guides who ever get to see it. And you'll no doubt want to float it as many times as you can before God and all your good living makes you too old and soft to make such a trip. As soon as I walked into the shop I saw the two lawyers who Larry guided last year. And then I saw the two docs I'd guided. I gave them a big hello and started over to them, but it seemed odd to me that Hank was standing with them instead of with his own clients. Wally stopped me before I could get halfway across the room and said, "Number Three, come here. I want you to meet your fishermen."

"I already know 'em," I said, pointing at the doctors.

"No you don't," said the walrus. He brought over these two young guys who couldn't, neither one of 'em, of been more than twenty-two or -three. One of 'em had hair as long as my old lady's, and each of 'em was wearing an earring that went right through his earlobe. They were both laughing and saying, "Glad to meet ya, Number Three," and I was too surprised by their ears to even tell them that Number Three is not my name, Goddamnit. They both shook my hand, which was an ordeal I can tell you, though they both had firm handshakes and not the melba toast kind of moist-palm, dishrag offering I was expecting.

We all stood around for a while talking about the Jones, and I told these boys they better be prepared for some bad weather and heavy water. They told me not to worry about them, but, believe me, I was. It turned out that my doctors, who Hank had stolen, were the fathers of these two boys. The trip with me was their present for graduating from college, where they had learned to wear jewelry like a damned woman and who knows what else. I wasn't happy with the situation and as soon as the clients went off to their motel, I jumped Wally about it.

Wally said that the doctors had asked for Hank, since his boat landed the most fish last year. He said Hank would be in charge of the trip. "I'm getting sick of your woman hating and your homophobia," he said, "so you can either take the job or quit. I'll find somebody else."

Did you ever hear such a bunch of bull in your life? I'm no woman hater. I just don't think they ought to be fishing. And I certainly ain't afraid of no homos. I probably should of quit old Wally right then and let him try to replace me, but I'm a loyal employee and I'm signed on for the season. So I just left the shop and came right home after only two beers at the Muddler.

Dear Piscatorial Partners,

A river will surprise you if you let it, and it is good to be surprised once in a while as long as you are in the capable hands of a professional guide.

The Jones River doesn't look like much at the put-in. The water doesn't have much "character," which is the word we professionals use for breaks in the flow like riffles or structure, such as rocks or snags or old cars, which fish can hide behind. The Daffodil is just filled with old cars and I catch a lot of fish near one old green Chevy that must of been a fine car before it fell in the river and became structure. But the Jones only has roads to the put-in and the take-out, which are sixty miles apart, except for a few ranch roads, which are private, so there are almost no cars in it where big trout can hide. Most ranchers seem to leave their old vehicles around their houses for windbreaks instead of putting them in the river for the fish. This makes sense because ranchers are all the time working and worrying about wheat or beef prices, and they have almost no time for the finer things of life like fly fishing. I'm just glad I was born with fish instead of cows in my blood.

This day the Jones was a little "off color," too, as the runoff was just beginning in the mountains. "Off color" is a term we professionals use to describe water that is not clear but is still fishable. Most clients call such water muddy, and get all disappointed before we even get started. So I was surprised when Steve—Steve and Mike were my clients—said, "This water is a little off color, Number Three, but I can still see down almost two feet. If it doesn't get any worse, we'll catch some fish."

That gave me a little hope, because I didn't expect these two longhairs to know anything at all about fishing. Apparently these boys' fathers, who being doctors had seen things the rest of us don't even want to imagine, had taught their sons an important fishing rule that you should all write down in your notebooks:

DON'T BE DISAPPOINTED BY AN UNEXPECTED COLOR OR APPARENT LACK OF CHARACTER.

The boys surprised me, too, by pitching right in to help load the rafts. The hardest part of floating the Jones is how long it always seems to take to actually get fishing. It's a five-hour drive to the put-in, and then it takes an hour or two to get all loaded up for the four-day float. My clients didn't seem to mind, though. Steve, who is taller than me and has long blond hair, is a lot stronger than he looks. He helped Elliott load the cargo raft while Mike, who is short and has dark hair and a gold earring, helped me. It looked like both of them had been around rafts before.

All the time we were working the boys were hollering at their fathers, saying they were gonna catch the most fish and the biggest fish. And by the time we actually put on the river Hank was holding a hundred dollars from each boat. The pot would go to the guide of the boat that landed the biggest fish. I would of give almost anything to trade clients with Hank, because I could sure use that three hundred and I didn't have a snowball's chance in a spring rain.

We sent Elliott on his way downriver first because it was his job, as cargo man, to set up camp and get the fire going and start cooking dinner. We all had some lunch while we let Elliott get a head start, and Hank's docs and my boys kept jabbering at each other about how bad they would outfish one another. Larry's clients were already drinking a lot of beer and they didn't like waiting. One of 'em went down to the river and began casting. He wasn't very good and he almost hooked Larry with his backcast. We use big weighted Woolly Buggers on the Jones and that really would of hurt. I like my beer, but there is no sense getting drunk on a beautiful and dangerous river. Hank saw what was going on so he decided we'd better get going. He pushed off first with Larry's boat following and my boat last. I didn't much like it, but it was the safest way to go so I didn't say much except to tell the boys that we would lead in the morning. "Hell," said Steve, "it's no problem. It's what we expected. They call you Number Three, don't they?"

I didn't say anything, just shoved off, and we were on our way. Steve fished from the bow and Mike from the stern. Neither one was a great caster but they had both fished before and they only hooked up with each other a couple of times. Steve caught a small brown in the first hundred yards and Mike lost a bigger one a few minutes later, so they both were smiling. We came around a lazy bend about an hour into the trip and we could hear hollering. I could see two rafts pulled up to the bank. Hank was standing on shore downriver from his raft hollering out at Elliott, who was in midriver playing a big fish. I could only hear a few words: "Goddamnit," "camp," "not fishing," and "for Christ's sake" rang out clear enough for everyone to know that Hank wasn't pleased.

"Hell," said Mike, "he ought to have a little fun, too." Steve agreed, and I found myself liking the boys better.

Elliott landed his fish, a good brown, waved it at Hank, released it, and rowed around the next bend. I rowed right past the boats on shore and pretended not to hear when Hank started yelling at me. It meant he'd have to take up the rear, which was where he belonged anyway. The boys were laughing and Mike mooned the doctors as we floated by. I laughed then, and when Steve caught a sixteen-inch brown right in front of his dad I figured it would be a damned good trip.

I forgot about the weather, though. The Jones River lives in a mountain canyon and the weather will surprise you every time. You have to pack sunscreen and winter clothes. We needed the winter stuff on the second day. I woke up early to find the tent settled down almost on my

nose. When I crawled out to pee and to help Elliott start
the fire I found our camp covered with four or five inches
of fresh snow. Another June day on the Jones.

Elliott already had the fire going. Hank had chewed
him out something terrible the night before, so I guess
Elliott wanted to keep him off his back today. He handed
me a cup of coffee and we sat near the fire not saying anything. A morning in the mountains doesn't need a lot of
jaw work. We hadn't been sitting there more than five
minutes when we heard a sound like a John Deere diesel
engine. Elliott pointed into the woods. There was a ruffed
grouse, all swelled up on his drumming log, his wings
beating too fast to see.

The boys and their fathers were up in time to see the
grouse, but Larry had to roust his clients out when breakfast was ready. They both poured whiskey in their coffee
and muttered about the damned weather. We set out with
Hank's boat leading, then Larry's, then mine. Elliott was
supposed to follow us until after lunch, when he would
go on ahead to set up camp.

I doubt those drunken lawyers saw the owl, even
though I could see Larry pointing at it through a heavy
snowfall. Owls are like bears. I mean, they're worth taking a minute to look at even if the fishing is good. And
the fishing was good. Steve had already caught an eigh-
teen-inch brown, but his dad had one that measured in at
twenty-two inches. So Hank's boat was leading for the
money. Larry's clients were spending most of the time

hunkered down, whining about the weather, so they weren't catching hardly any fish. Mike hooked into what I figured would of been the big winner just as I made the mistake of pointing out the owl. He got to looking at that bird, forgot to keep his line tight, and lost that monster fish.

I almost don't blame him, though. A man doesn't see an owl very often. Elliott says that's because they are nocturnal creatures, but I told him I didn't care about that.

"Elliott," I said, "all you seem to care about is sex. I don't give a hoot about the sex life of birds and the world would be a better place if nobody else did either. Besides, I think there aren't many owls because an owl doesn't have much time for that sort of thing, being up all night hunting the way he is."

This owl was a big one—one of them great horned owls that doesn't really have horns, but only looks like it does. He reminded me of the devil, staring out at us with those big yellow eyes. He never moved at all, except his head, and without a true woodsman like yours truly along these boys wouldn't of spotted him at all. We couldn't stop, though, because it is right where this owl was perched that the Jones starts to pick up speed and roar down through the canyon with lots of fast water and bends that go right up against the canyon wall.

We were well into the first bend when I took my eyes away from that owl. The damned bird had no doubt hypnotized me. We still would of been okay if Steve had given me more warning, but he waited until the last minute to yell, "Look out!" So the raft whacked up against this big old rock that had no business being where it was.

We didn't really hit it very hard. I managed to keep my seat and to catch the oar that came out of the cheap oarlock (which Wally insists on buying) before it hit the water. So everything would of been fine, except Mike, who was sitting in the stern, must of been watching that devil of an owl instead of paying attention. So he got his fool self tossed out of the raft.

He was wearing his life jacket but it's still not a good idea to let yourself get thrown into the Jones River in June, because the water is cold and fast and rolly, and there are a lot of rocks in there, like the one Steve let me hit. Things were fast and furious there for a few minutes. Steve was yelling and looking like he might jump out of the raft so I had to tell him to stay put, while I was trying to jam the oar back on that cheap oarlock. By the time I got the oar back on we were in a back eddy and Mike was downstream ahead of us. I'd of caught him all right, but Elliott went by us pushing his raft through the rapids for all he was worth. I still don't know how an inexperienced oarsman like him got there so fast, but he did. The next thing I knew he had grabbed ahold of Mike and dragged him over the side of the raft. For a guy with a wimpy name, Elliott is some kind of strong.

Larry must of seen the whole thing and he must of squealed to Hank, because both boats were pulled over

and waiting for us around the next bend. They already had
a fire started, and as soon as we got there they had Mike
strip his clothes off, and put him in a sleeping bag to warm
up, and had Steve get in there with him (which I didn't
think was necessary). But it worked. It wasn't long before
Mike was dressed and warm and we'd all had some lunch
and were ready to go fishing. The doctors and everybody
else were making a big fuss over Elliott like he was some
kind of hero. Nobody was even talking to me.

We were almost ready to go and I gave Mike one of
my fly rods to use because he had lost his head and let go
of his in the river. Hank had been talking to the two doctors and he came over to my raft. Right off, he told Mike
he could keep the fly rod I had given him. That pissed me
off some and the only thing that saved Hank's bacon was
that I have a rule about never fighting in front of clients.
Then he walked me away from the raft and told me that
the doctors wouldn't allow their sons to go any farther
down the river with me rowing. You'd of thought it was
my fault the fool kid fell in the drink.

Hank said that Elliott would row my raft the rest of
the way and I would row the cargo raft. I said it would be
a cold day in hell before I rowed any damned garbage
scow, but Hank said it was either that or I could walk out.
I'll get him for that someday. He was just making sure he'd
win that three hundred dollars.

There isn't much more to say about the trip down
the Jones, because I know that all you are interested in is

fishing and I wasn't doing any of that. I just rowed the cargo raft and set up camp and got dinner ready. I didn't fool around with any fishing like Elliott had done, because anything I do, I do it good. I guess the boys caught a lot of fish, even with Elliott rowing, or at least they said so to make him feel good. But Steve's dad still had the lead with that twenty-two-inch brown. Elliott and the boys tried to cheer me up at camp and let me know that there was no hard feelings, but I just did my job and went to bed early, leaving them all laughing at the campfire.

The last day on the Jones is always a lazy one. The river flows out of the canyon and enters some farmland. The fishing usually slows down just like the river, but sometimes you can catch a good rainbow in this stretch. I had broke camp after the rest of the boats left and pushed down the river until I met them where they stopped for lunch. It was a warm, sunny day and we were all standing around watching a pair of bald eagles in a cottonwood tree across the river when Mike decided to wade out and try his luck one more time. He hadn't made more than half a dozen casts with a big olive Woolly Bugger when he hooked a huge fish. It was a good thing he had lost his fly rod and had my good one or he probably never would of landed the monster. Elliott waded out to Mike and netted the creature. Then we all laughed: It was a damned carp. But Mike insisted on measuring it—it was twenty-six inches long and had to weigh more than most babies. There was a big argument after that, but it was no doubt the biggest fish of the trip. Even though doctors are supposed to be smart, they hadn't thought to make the bet for the biggest trout. So Elliott got the three hundred dollars. I wouldn't of took the money for no bottom-feeding carp, but some guys have no pride at all.

On the ride home Elliott handed me $150, saying he would feel better that way. I took it, only to make him feel better.

DEAR PISCATORIAL PARTNERS,

I should probably call you Pugilistic Partners today. At least that's what Nancy thinks. She is sometimes as weird about the American language as Elliott. She is also sick. She is even more hung over than I am after our night at the Muddler and has gone back to bed after taking another look at my eye, which is swelled shut, and my nose, which might be broke again on account of that logger getting lucky and getting behind me like he did. But I'm getting ahead of myself, so I'll start at the beginning.

We all went to the Muddler last night to celebrate our successful trip on the Jones River. Murphy was tending bar. Elliott and I challenged Mike and Steve to a game of pool, and we lost ten bucks because Elliott can't keep his attention on the game and tried to talk to me when I was shooting the eight ball in the corner pocket off a double bank. I scratched, which means we lost. The boys wanted to play again but I didn't want to trust Elliott with any more of my money, so Elliott and I joined the women.

Beth had surprised Elliott by being here when we got back from the Jones. She said she had frequent flier miles and wanted to take another look at the place, which I took to mean she wanted another look at Elliott. Elliott seemed glad to see her but confused, too, like a guy is when fish are rising all around him but he can't figure out what they're feeding on. Nancy and Beth were getting along great and, at one point, I even remember Beth telling

Nancy that they ought to go fishing sometimes and that she would teach her how to cast and row and everything, and Nancy surprised the hell out of me by saying she would like to do that. That's when I knew she was getting drunk, and I'm sure she has forgotten all about it this morning. Just the same, I'm glad Beth is going back to Vermont tomorrow.

Anyway, I was listening to this silly conversation and I didn't notice these four loggers come in and gather around the pool table until Elliott nudged me with an elbow. There's still a lot of loggers around here and some of 'em are even my friends. But they ain't by nature a friendly lot and I knew they wouldn't like the boys, because they wore earrings, even though you won't find no better men than Mike and Steve.

One of the loggers is called Burdock, because he wears wool pants, even in the summer, and they are always covered with sticky weeds. He challenged Mike to a game for the rights to the table.

"Hey, little girl," he said, "I'll play you for the table."

Good ol' Mike never backed down. He said, "The table and ten bucks."

"Who do you think you're shitting?" said Burdock. "You're on! Go ahead and break 'em."

Mike broke 'em, all right, and put the three ball in the corner to boot. Then he ran the table, called the eight ball in the corner, sank it sweet as your sister, and said, "Thanks for the game. You owe me ten bucks."

It ain't often anybody runs the table at the Muddler. Burdock stood there with his mouth hanging open like there was swallows in there wanting to fly out. He finally stammered, "The hell I do. I ain't getting hustled by no longhair."

I guess I better stop right here and admit that old Burdock didn't really say no such thing. What Burdock really said would peel the paint off the church down on Hickory Street that a whole passel of us got together and painted just two years ago. But I refuse to write down such language even if it was old Burdock's mouth those filthy words came out of.

It was time to go into action. I could see that my friends were up that well-known creek without a paddle and needing my help. So I jumped off the bar stool and headed towards Burdock saying, "Hey, you!" or something like that.

My daddy always told me not to shoot off my mouth in a fight. "If the feces is gonna fly, boy, you might just as well throw the first punch. It might turn out to be the last one."

So I was ready, and I wasn't gonna do no more talking. But old Burdock's daddy must of taught him the same thing because he didn't even answer me, just busted me one right over the left eye. It wasn't much of a punch and wouldn't of amounted to a hill of ants, but it hit some veins or arteries or something that our eyes are just full of. It's all swelled up this morning like I fell in a hive of hornets. The bad part was that the punch sort of turned me around and ol' Burdock, who is not much of a fighter but who is a big galoot, was able to jump on my back and knock me to the floor. He started punching me in the back of the head and somewhere in there I banged my nose and it started bleeding. Hell was breaking loose all around me, and I just wanted to get this big lummox off me and help the boys with the rest of the fight. I was sure Elliott wouldn't be much help.

Some of the next facts were told to me by Nancy while she was applying ice from her gin and tonic to my nose and eye after things had calmed down a bit.

I guess Elliott had followed right behind me and as soon as ol' Burdock jumped me, Elliott threw a beautiful punch at one of the other tree killers and felled him. "Timber," I heard Nancy holler, and I knew she'd had enough gin.

Steve was even more of a surprise. I wish I'd made quicker work of ol' Burdock so as I could of seen him in action. We learned later that Steve was a Golden Gloves fighter and had boxed all the time he was in college. He just played with this huge guy who Murphy said had squeezed a guy almost to death in a fight a couple of months back. Murphy said that watching Steve cut this big logger up with his fists was like watching a wolverine destroy a grizzly bear, which I read about once but didn't really believe. Anyhow, I'm sorry I missed it, but while Steve was playing Cassius Clay I was starting to get my elbows and knees under me and would no doubt soon of been on my feet and showing ol' Burdock a thing or two, but Elliott once again spoiled my fun. As soon as he had knocked his guy down for the third time he turned and kicked ol' Burdock in the side of the head and knocked him senseless.

I sat up and rubbed the blood out of my eyes just in time to watch the women rescue Mike from this logger who only has the name Skinner as far as I know and who doesn't waste much time taking baths. Mike is a pool shark and a poet and not much given to fighting, so he needed some help.

Skinner had a hold of Mike's hair. Mike will learn one of these days that, if you are going to be a man in this world and fish and fight and stuff, having long hair is a good way to get yourself killed. In fact, I wouldn't be surprised to find him in Clayton's barber chair this very afternoon, except for the fact that his whole head probably hurts too much to have anybody touch it.

Anyway, Skinner held Mike by the hair and was punching him in the face with his other hand. I guess it wasn't a pretty sight and it got the womenfolk all upset. So just as I stood up and begun to clear my head and look to see who I should tackle next, Nancy and Beth ran up to old Skinner and pushed him away from Mike. Beth got a hold of Mike, as soon as Skinner let go, and squirreled him away from there. But my old lady had gin in her veins and rage in her heart. She shoved Skinner one more time.

That worthless tree murderer, who has no respect for women or nobody, shoved back, and my Nancy fell to the floor.

Elliott and I were both yelling and heading for Skinner, but I got there first. I hope Steve was watching, because he could of learned something to put in his Golden Glove. When I got to Skinner I didn't say nothing, I just started in with a left jab. I'm right-handed, but I threw a left at Skinner's chin to set him up for a right hook. I guess I was too mad, though, because my aim was off. Instead of busting Skinner one on the chin or on the end of the nose, I hit him in the Adam's apple. I must nearly of made applesauce out of it, too, because my right hook hit nothing but air. Skinner was down on the floor making funny noises, clutching his throat and kicking his legs around. The fight was over.

Murphy finally came out from behind the bar with his ball bat and threw all the loggers out. It took two of them to help Skinner out of the place, I had whupped him so bad. Murphy said to me, "Jesus, Donnie, I thought I was gonna have to throw your ass out of here," which shows that he wasn't watching close and didn't see that I was about to get the best of ol' Burdock without any help from Elliott.

You see, Murphy has rules at the Muddler. He knows that there will be fights sometimes, and he won't never call the cops unless somebody pulls a gun or a knife. He just throws the losers out for two weeks. He claims he'd rather have winners in his bar and he doesn't want no grudge fight rematches. He also throws anybody who has two fights in the same month out of the bar for a month, so me and Elliott will have to watch our Ps and Qs for a while. Nancy says it'll take a month for my face to heal anyway, but she's wrong. It would take more than the likes of Burdock to hurt me, though I'll say that I am glad it's Sunday. I think I'll take a nap, and then go over to the shop to see who I'll be guiding this week.

DEAR PARTNERS,

DON'T NEVER TRUST YOUR BOSS ESPECIALLY IF YOU ONCE THOUGHT HE WAS YOUR BEST FRIEND.

That is the tip today and it really isn't a fishing tip, just the same as I didn't call you my Piscatorial Partners, because I am no longer working for Wally and am at present an unemployed fishing guide, right in the middle of the fishing season, because Wally went and fired me. Oh, I'm sure he'll soon see that he can't run his business without his best guide and will come begging me to come back to work, maybe as soon as this afternoon. But it will be like talking into the wind in hurricane season, because I am through with him, and with Elliott, too, as once more Elliott has backstabbed me and is the man Wally says he is hiring to take my place. It is not a fair world, and it is discouraging.

DEAR FRIENDS,

It's hard to call you Piscatorial Partners when I haven't done any fishing for almost two weeks. I wasn't going to write anymore either, since I am unfairly unemployed and unable to call myself a professional guide. I haven't even been tying flies. The whole idea of having Wally make any more money off my hard labors makes me sick to my stomach. I have been spending most of my time out at my shop whittling. Whittling is something I have done since I was about five years old and my daddy gave me my first knife. I whittle birds. It's just a hobby and nothing to talk about to serious fishermen, and I wouldn't even be mentioning it now except that my shop is where Elliott found me when he brought out the latest issue of your newsletter.

It no doubt surprises you that I even let Elliott on my property, what with him taking my job and everything. And I don't blame you. This was the first time he has ever been here, and I probably would of run him off if he hadn't snuck up on me in the shop. He knocked at the door and, being involved in whittling the eye of an owl like I was, I just hollered, "Come in," and there he was.

I didn't know what to say, except, "What the hell are you doing here?"

Elliott didn't even answer me. He just stood there looking around and ended up staring at me like he'd never seen me before. My shop isn't very big—just an old shed I made when I took over the old house. It has a workbench with a vise and anvil and a grindstone. And it has a good woodstove so it's a comfortable place to work even in the heart of Montana's heartless winters. Like I said, I was working on an owl so that bird was in my hand, but Elliott walked over to the heron I just finished last week. It is my biggest project ever, and I started it the day after Elliott and I first went fishing on the Daffodil. It's altogether about four feet high and has this great blue heron landing in the topmost branch of an old cottonwood tree. It's too big to bring into the house, and I really don't even know why I made that overgrown old fish eater. I usually just do songbirds and hummingbirds and such, and the old lady, I mean Nancy, has them all over the house.

Anyway, Elliott was running his fingers over some of the feathers I had whittled into that heron. He said, "Number Three, I didn't know you were an artist."

"I am an artist with a fly rod," I said. "This is just whittling and is something a man does to waste time when some out-of-stater has stole his job."

Elliott ain't no fool and he knew better than to say anything about that. He just took the owl out of my hand and looked at it. Then he asked me if I had any other bird carvings.

"They are just whittling," I said. But nothing would do but that I bring him into the house and show him some of the other birds. So I gave him a beer, even though he is no longer my friend, and let him wander around the house. My daddy was a carpenter and he taught me a lot, so the house is all wood floors and homemade shelves and stuff. Elliott seemed surprised and kept going on about how impressed he was to see what he called my handiwork, but then I guess all the houses in New York must be made out of bricks or cement since you likely don't have any trees big enough for lumber.

Elliott mostly liked the birds, though. Before I could stop him he had a bunch of them out in the front yard and was taking pictures with the camera that follows him everywhere he goes. I just sat in the kitchen and read your newsletter and drank beer and prayed we would get all the birds back where they belonged before my old lady got home and pitched a fit. She came home, though, while Elliott was taking pictures, and the two of them talked quite a while. I figured she was probably chewing on him good so I just opened another Pabst Blue Ribbon and sat there in the kitchen reading a whole bunch of lies in your paper about the brown trout fishing in New Zealand being the best in the world. When Nancy came in the door she was smiling and said she had invited Elliott to stay for dinner, which just goes to show that women sometimes have no sense at all.

She lost her mind again during dinner when Elliott mentioned that he had the next day off. She suggested that Elliott and I go fishing together.

Elliott said, "How about it, Number Three?"

I would of rather had a nervous breakdown, but I couldn't make my wife look bad. So Elliott and I'll fish tomorrow and I'll have something to write about again.

Your newsletter was okay. But you cut out some of the stuff that showed how it was Mike's own fault that he ended up in the drink. And I didn't think you should of run the ad from the Barbless now that you understand what a backstabber Wally is.

DEAR PISCATORIAL PARTNERS,

Elliott and I got into it again today. We were driving up to Stony Creek when he said, "Number Three, I know you like to think that the fishing in Montana is deteriorating because of all the nonresident fishermen, but the truth of it is that your rivers have a lot of silt in them from past and present mining practices and agricultural operations, and most of your spawning beds are too full of silt to be productive."

That's what a lot of people are saying, but most of 'em are out-of-staters and don't understand life out here in the West. Loggers and ranchers and miners have to feed their families the same as fishing guides. There were miners here when I was a boy and the fishing was damn good then. I think these newcomers just want the land for themselves. But I am sick of arguing about it to people who just don't get it.

So I told Elliott, "Our fishing is not deteriorating. There's just not as many big fish in the rivers as there used to be, because there are so many out-of-staters standing in every fishable run. It's not fair to blame the miners. I know a few of them and they are not down there practicing but are real professionals just like yours truly. The ones I know don't even hardly fish. They spend so much time underground that their eyes are sensitive to the light so they spend most of their time, when they aren't working, at the Muddler, where the light is dim and they can see what they're doing. And the only agricultural operation I know about is when the Talbot boy ran a four-wheeler into a barbed wire fence on his daddy's ranch and the doctors took four hours to sew him back together. That was a bad day but I don't see how it hurt the fishing none."

Elliott didn't have nothing to say when I was done, just like I knew he wouldn't. Anyway, we were almost to one of my favorite spots on Stony Creek so we quit arguing, which probably saved Elliott's bacon yet again. The fishing really wasn't much to talk about so I won't waste your time with it, except to say we only caught five fish all afternoon—which might seem like a good day to you people in New York, but which don't count for much of nothing here.

P.S.—Elliott just read this and he said I don't want to talk about the fishing because he caught four of the five fish, but that is hogwash as you must know by now. Five fish is hardly nothing, and even if Elliott did catch one that went probably four pounds, it was just beginner's luck.

DEAR PISCATORIAL PARTNERS,

As you have no doubt already figured, this is about the worst summer I have spent since I took up the noble profession of guiding fishermen down our great western rivers. But Larry's season is even worse. Not only did he get to guide two drunks on the Jones River but, just yesterday, he jumped off his pickup truck while loading his raft and broke his ankle. I know this because Wally called me today and offered me my job back.

Well, I'm sure you know me well enough by now to know that I would of told him to go to hell in a handbasket except for the fact that my old lady likes to have three meals a day and can't seem to stay away from the grocery store. I made him sweat a little and then I told him I'd come back, but only if I got first pick on all clients.

He said, "I'm only calling you because Elliott thought I should and because I've known you so long. You'll get clients after all the other boats are full. And if you have another accident or get in another brawl, you'll never again work for me or any other outfitter in this town."

Can you believe that? You'd think it was my fault that fool kid fell out of the raft. I wanted to get in another brawl right then—with Wally. But the old lady had started cooking things like liver and onions and tuna and white gravy, so I knew she was hinting that I better get back to work. So I'll be floating the Daffodil tomorrow with Hank and Elliott and some brand-new clients. I'm supposed to pick Elliott up on my way to Trudy's.

DEAR PISCATORIAL PARTNERS,

EVERYBODY KNOWS THE EARLY BIRD GETS THE WORM. SO IT STANDS TO REASON THAT A FISHERMAN SHOULD NOT LET ANY GRASS GROW UNDER HIS BED, BUT SHOULD BE UP AND CASTING HIS FLY BEFORE THE TROUT ARE FULL OF WORMS AND ARE NO LONGER INTERESTED IN THE HIGHER ORDER OF INSECTS.

I really let the doorbell blast the fourth time I rang it. Elliott answered the door and he was still in his underwear. "Let's go fishing," I said.

"Number Three! It's only six A.M., for Christ's sake."

"Yeah, time's a-wasting. Let's get going."

Well, Elliott turned on a light and told me to make myself at home, which was not very easy to do as I already had my waders on. Elliott went back to his room to change and I heard some woman ask what the hell was going on. I was surprised, because I didn't think Beth was back in town. Anyway, it didn't sound like Beth's voice. But I am not one to pry up the business of friends, so I just quit listening.

This was the first time I had been in Elliott's apartment. I wasn't being nosy, but it was taking Elliott forever to get dressed and I couldn't sit long in those waders, so I just sort of wandered around looking the place over. I ended up at the bookshelf. I am more interested in books since I've become a writer, and Elliott has more books than he does good sense. Not a one of 'em that I saw was about fishing, though, and I was fast losing interest when I saw this picture frame that had accidentally got turned around facing the wall.

Naturally, I turned it back the way it belonged. I was looking at a picture of Elliott and this pretty woman I figured right away must be his wife back in New York. I decided that because there were two kids in the picture—a young girl, maybe seven or eight years old, who was blonde and looked a lot like the woman standing next to Elliott, and a boy about twelve who was the spitting image of Elliott, only shorter. I was some surprised. I can tell you that right up front. Here Elliott was supposed to be my best friend and he had never told me he had kids. I remembered, though, how quiet he got way back in May when I asked him if he was married, so I decided to leave well enough alone. Besides, I could still hear that woman in his bedroom who was not Beth and was damn sure not his wife. It didn't seem like a good time to ask Elliott about his family. I turned the picture back against the wall. Elliott came out carrying his fly rod and those damned worthless hip boots of his and we went to pick up our clients.

It was not a great day on the Daffodil, at least not by Montana standards. Each raft landed maybe a dozen fish, but nobody caught any lunkers. My clients were okay, though I spent my whole tip in the Muddler on the way home so you can see that generosity was not their middle name. Still, it's great to be working and to feel like a true professional once more.

DEAR PISCATORIAL PARTNERS,

Just because tomorrow is the Fourth of July doesn't mean that independence has to be in the air where every fool woman can breathe it and think she owns it.

Beth is back in town, has been for three days. She called Nancy last week all the way from Burlington, Vermont, and they talked for almost fifteen minutes, which just goes to show you that lawyers have no respect for money. When Nance hung up she was smiling. "Beth is coming back July first for two months; maybe she'll even decide to move here."

She sounded excited, but I don't much like her hanging around that female lawyer who is single and has no sense of responsibility. "Doesn't that woman ever work?" I said. "She better stick to being a lawyer instead of chasing out here trying to marry poor ol' Elliott who is already married."

"Donnie Phillips, you don't know what you're talking about. Beth is not chasing after Elliott. She likes him, all right, but she's coming out here because she's sick of working in a law firm run by her father and her older brother. She wants to prove she can make it on her own and has taken a two-month leave of absence so she can look for opportunities."

Well, Montana is not the land of opportunity for anybody except fishing guides and loggers, and I still say that Beth has her sights set on Elliott. But I didn't say nothing more, except to tell my old lady I didn't want Beth hanging around here all the time. You'll no doubt understand why when I finish telling you what happened today.

Elliott and I worked hard today, guiding four guys down the Lewis Spoon who couldn't catch fish in a barrel with worms and a bobber. It was a long day and, at the end of it, Elliott drove me home. I just wanted to go have a beer in the backyard but we could see Beth was there, so Elliott stayed. Beth and Nancy were standing in the kitchen looking like pups what had stole the bacon, so I knew they had been into the gin and tonics again. They called us over to look in the sink to see what was for dinner so, after I took a couple of Pabst Blue Ribbons out of the refrigerator, we went over to humor them. The way Nancy has been feeding me lately I expected eggplant or some other indelible vegetable, but instead there were four rainbow trout in the sink. Beth said that every one of them was over fourteen inches long, but I would like to know who taught women to measure.

What I really wanted to know was why these women were off buying trout that was probably raised in some pond by farmers who didn't know how to grow wheat when their men were professional fishermen. Nancy said, "We didn't buy them, Number Three, we caught them. Beth caught three and I caught one."

Well, if she hadn't of been drinking gin, and if we hadn't of had company, I guess you know I never would of allowed my wife to call me Number Three. But I didn't say anything, just sat down at the table while Nance and Beth interrupted each other all over the place telling us how they had rented a raft at Hoolihan's and had spent the day floating the Daffodil, with Beth teaching Nance how to cast a fly rod and even how to row.

I couldn't believe it. Hoolihan's is this old store downtown owned by a guy of the same name who used to run a good honest pawnshop, but who now rents rafts and other sporting equipment to amateurs and neophytes and all sorts of weird people who think they can master our rivers without hiring a guide. We guides call it Hooligan's and we can hardly wait until somebody drowns in one of those rafts and sues ol' Hooligan and puts him out of business. Now my own old lady had gone and rented one of his rafts.

"You damn fools! You could of been drowned," was all I managed to say.

"We didn't drown, silly man," said Nancy, trying to give me a hug. "We had fun, and we're going to do it again."

"That will be a cold day in hell," I said.

"It'll be next Saturday, and we'll float the Lewis Spoon and learn some new water."

"Yeah," chipped in Beth, "we already reserved our raft."

"I am the only one in this family who needs to be risking his life learning new water and I won't have my wife drowning because some female lawyer thinks she knows all about everything."

"Come on, Number Three," said Elliott, "you know Beth can handle a raft. Nobody's gonna drown in these rivers in the middle of the summer, anyway."

That goes to show you what kind of a friend Elliott is. Just when you give him one of your Pabst Blue Ribbons like you would a real pal, he turns on you, and tries to turn your old lady on you and maybe get her drowned to boot. I told him to mind his own damned business; then I went into the bedroom to take off my waders.

When I came out Elliott and the women were out at the barbecue, so I grabbed a cold Pabst and joined them. Just as I walked up Beth said, "Elliott, I've given it a lot of thought, and I've decided to move my practice here. I like it here, and this town could use a woman in the bar."

Once more it was time for me to save Elliott's bacon. I could see he didn't know what to say, so I told Beth right out what I thought.

"Beth, that's not a very good idea. Murphy won't stand for no woman butting into his profession. This town just isn't big enough for that. And I don't understand why you want to practice tending bar when you already know how to be a female lawyer."

Beth started laughing so hard she ended up rolling around on the ground, which just goes to show you that she can't hold her gin and has no business working in a barroom.

Nancy was laughing, too. Seems, according to Nance, Beth plans to practice law out here. Ralph Donaldson has already offered her a job while she gets ready to take her Montana bar exams. In September she'll go back to Burlington, Vermont, to tie things up. "By January," Beth said, "I'll be living here full time."

She put her arm around Nancy, then, and they looked happier than a pair of possums in a corn patch.

I can't say the news tickled me all that much but I just drank my beer and kept quiet. Nancy took my arm and said, "I have even better news. Let's go for a walk."

I was worried about dinner but Beth said she'd watch the fish, so Nance and I took a walk. There's almost ten acres of land on this piece of property that used to be my father's, so even with our house and my shop there's lots of room to walk. Before we got ten feet away, though, I heard Beth say, "Don't worry, Elliott. I've rented an apartment."

"I . . . I . . . I guess you could, ah . . . ah . . . live with me."

Nancy tried to get me to walk faster but I was worried about Elliott who I had never heard stutter before, so I held my ground. Nobody paid attention to me. Beth just took Elliott's hand. "Look, Elliott," she said. "I think we'd better just be friends. You have some unfinished business back in New York. Besides, you're sowing some wild oats right now. That's okay. But I don't need to be involved with a man like that."

I felt better then and let Nancy drag me away. We hadn't walked more than fifty feet when Nancy dropped a bomb right on my world. I'll tell you about it but first I'll advise you, if you are single, to stay that way.

IT TAKES MORE THAN BEING A FIRST-CLASS FISHERMAN AND RIVER GUIDE TO SATISFY A WOMAN.

That is the sad truth. Even when life is almost perfect, a woman is never satisfied and is always wanting to change things. And if you let two of them get together and one is a lawyer, you'll have hell to pay. I can tell you that.

Nancy said, "Donnie, what would you think about building another house on the property?"

"What the hell would we do with another house?"

She said she and Beth had been talking and they had come up with a plan.

"I know you've been talking," I said. "And I aim to put an end to that. I don't want you hanging around that female ambulance chaser anymore."

"Donnie Phillips, you don't know what the hell you're talking about. Just for once shut up and listen. Beth has some money put aside and she wants to invest it. We figure we could build a lodge on this property to hold six or eight guests—kind of a bed-and-breakfast idea, only we would cater to men and women who want to fish. Beth would be the outfitter, and we'd have guides like you and

Elliott, but also some women guides. I might even be one myself."

That was the damnedest notion I had heard in my life and I said so in no uncertain terms. Then Beth hollered out that dinner was ready. We ate the fish, to give meaning to their dead lives, but I didn't feel much like eating. I bet Elliott didn't, neither. These women had turned our lives upside down. After dinner I went into the house to write this, and now I am going to bed so I won't have to talk about it anymore.

DEAR PISCATORIAL PARTNERS,

If the original Fourth of July had been as big a bust for those fighting Pilgrims as this one was for Elliott and me, we would all still be slaves on British plantations, drinking tea instead of coffee, and, no doubt, casting with both hands.

Elliott and Beth were supposed to meet us at the Muddler, but I didn't expect to see them.

"If I was old Elliott I wouldn't give that woman the time of day, Nancy. She practically told him she never wanted to see him again."

"Donnie Phillips, she never said any such thing. She was just letting him know that he better figure things out before she would invest any more energy in him."

"I sure as hell never heard her say anything like that."

"That's the trouble with you men. You only hear what you want to hear."

"Well, I sure as hell don't want to hear nothing about no bread-and-breakfast with women guiding men down the river."

Nancy started laughing. Don't it make you mad as hell when a woman starts laughing right in the middle of an argument, like maybe she knows something you don't?

She said, "Silly man, it's bed-and-breakfast, not bread-and-breakfast."

"Damnit all, Nance, don't go making it worse than it already is. It's a hair-brained idea that only some woman with a law degree could cook up because she's of no use in the kitchen."

Nancy had that look in her eye that usually means I'm going to sleep on the couch, and that's a hell of a way to celebrate the birth of a nation that includes states as great as Montana.

Right then Beth and Elliott walked through the door of the Muddler like they belonged together. It was maybe the first time in my life I was ever glad to see Elliott. But, as you no doubt expect by now, it didn't last long. He ordered two Pabst Blue Ribbons and two gin and tonics from Murph and the first damned words out of his mouth were, "Say, Number Three, Beth has been telling me about this new bed-and-breakfast fishing lodge idea. Sounds like a winner to me."

Elliott wouldn't know a winner if he was sitting astraddle old Sweet William, the horse that won most of the races at last year's county fair, but before I could tell him so my lovely wife piped up in the most sarcastic voice I have ever heard: "Donnie doesn't think women belong on our *dangerous* Montana rivers."

"Number Three," Elliott said. "Beth canoed most of the major rivers in the East when she was a member of Cornell's Outing Club. She has solo canoed on such famous white-water rivers as the Raquette and the West Branch of the Delaware. She also worked as a guide for her uncle who is an outfitter on Michigan's Upper Peninsula. So I don't think you have to worry about Beth's credentials."

"I'm not worried about her credentials. And the way things look between you two, I guess you can forget about them, too. But nothing you've said has convinced me that the woman can run a raft down the Daffodil without getting somebody killed."

"Don't forget, Number Three," butted in Beth, "that I rowed you down Stony Creek in high water. As I recall, nobody died that day."

"Be quiet!" I growled at her, looking around to see if Hank or, worse, Wally had heard her. The Muddler was starting to fill up, because Murph had hired a group called "The Old Timey Fiddle Fools" so people could dance and be entertained on the Fourth of July.

"Listen, Beth," I said in a low voice like I'd use to tell a friend where the fishing was good, "I made a mistake that day, and I'm man enough to admit it. We lucked out and you didn't drown none of us, but it won't happen again. And it's not a good thing to talk about in a place like the Muddler, if you get my drift."

Well, that lawyer woman told me I was drifting up a well-known creek without a paddle. I won't name that creek just like I haven't given the real name of any other creeks or rivers. The fiddlers were tuning up so we didn't talk much more, except that Beth challenged Elliott and me to a fishing contest.

She said, "I've got a proposition for you, Number Three. The next time Wally gives you and Elliott a day off, Nance and I will rent a raft from Hoolihan's and we'll float any river you name. I bet we land more fish from our boat than you two do from yours. Are you game?"

I said, "Sure, why not?" You see, it's the middle of the tourist season and a dead man's cinch that neither Elliott nor I'll have another day off until probably October. Besides, there's no way Nance can miss any more work to go fishing with this mixed-up female. And Elliott and Beth are close to being past tense, if you'll allow me to use writer's language. So it's a safe bet that nothing will come of all these foolish ideas.

The band got to cooking, and Nance and I started dancing. Beth and Elliott moved to a table in the back of the Muddler and, for most of an hour, they had their heads together talking. Then Beth got up and left without even coming over to say good-bye. Five minutes later Elliott was dancing with Violet Anderson, who everybody knows is newly divorced.

I should of just kept dancing but instead I went and opened my mouth. I said, "Well, look at that, Nance. I guess your lawyer friend will give up all her ideas about staying here and becoming a fishing guide now that Elliott has seen the light and told her off. I bet she leaves town tomorrow and we never see her again."

Nancy said, "Donnie Phillips, you don't know what you're effing talking about." And then she stormed out the door of the Muddler without even waiting for midnight, when we'd all go outside to watch the fireworks from the banks of the Lewis Spoon River.

Now before you literate types get all excited, I know that "effing" is not a word. It's not even what my old lady really said. But it is as close as I will utter to the real word. I don't know what got into Nancy, using a word like that. But if you are a language purist and don't like "effing" and want to see the real McCoy in print, you'll have to go to one of those "adults only" stores with the shades all pulled down on the windows and doors. There are two of them right here in town, so there are probably six or seven in a place the size of New York.

Anyway, after Nancy left, I just sat there drinking another Pabst Blue Ribbon and listening to the music. I wanted to dance some more, it being the Fourth of July and all, but I am faithful to my old lady and not like Elliott. A bit before midnight, I bought a six-pack of Pabst from Murph. Usually the old lady and I like to snuggle down by the big rock and watch the fireworks, so I wasn't all that happy. I figured I might as well go home and have another beer or two and sleep on the couch.

But Elliott must of seen me buy that six-pack, because he was standing next to me before I could even turn and walk out the door. "Come on, Number Three, let's go watch the fireworks."

"I thought you were with Violet Anderson."

"Oh, she just asked me to dance. I have to learn to say no."

"That's not all you have to learn."

"You're right about that, Number Three."

We went down to the big rock where we watched the fireworks and drank my whole six-pack so I didn't end up with any to take home. But it was okay. Elliott wanted to talk, and fireworks aren't so exciting that you can't listen to a friend so long as he is willing to let you interrupt and say, "Ooh, look at that one," once in a while.

Elliott said that he wanted to talk about Beth if I didn't mind. He said, "Beth is a damned good woman. I like to think we'd make a good team. I'm just not very available right now."

"Not available!" I said. "You sure can't tell that from looking."

"I guess you've got a point there, Number Three. What I mean is . . . Well, I guess I haven't really told you very much about myself. I told you I'm separated from my wife. But it's worse than that. I have two kids back home in New York."

I knew that, of course, but it seemed like a good time to drink my Pabst Blue Ribbon and just let Elliott talk. He talked for a long time, and I won't put everything he said in this article, as most of it didn't have much to do with fishing. Still, a man brings his whole self to the river, so maybe more of life is about fishing than we really know.

**IT IS NOT A PERFECT WORLD, SO NONE OF
US GET TO GO FISHING ALL THE TIME.**

Anyway, Elliott was really missing his kids that night, said he missed them most all the time. I asked him if his son liked to fish but he said no, his daughter was the one he took fishing. His boy likes music. That worried me some until he said the whole family did a lot of hiking in the Adirondack Mountains. I can't imagine there being a very long trail in a place as crowded as New York, but I could see Elliott was not in the mood to argue so I didn't bring it up.

Elliott said that he thought he had it all figured out when he left New York. He was just surprised that he missed them all so much. "Hell," he said, "I even miss my wife, and I know that's over."

I handed him another Pabst Blue Ribbon. "New York isn't Mars," I said. "Why don't you just pack 'em up and move 'em out here? The old lady and I might be able to loan you some money if that's the problem."

Elliott drank some beer. "That's not the problem. I wish it was, but thanks just the same. You're a good friend, Number Three." Elliott stood up then and just walked away in the dark.

I finished watching the fireworks and drank the rest of my last beer. Then I walked on home. It was nearly two A.M. so I snuck in real quiet. But I needn't of bothered. Nancy wasn't home. There was a message on that phone machine she insisted we buy saying she was spending the night with Beth, who needed someone to talk to. Everybody needed to talk. I could of slept in the bed but I took a blanket from the closet and slept on the couch. I figured that was the way it would of been if Nancy had been home.

DEAR PISCATORIAL PARTNERS,

It has been so long since I last wrote to you that nearly the entire month of July has wilted on the vine. It is too damned hot. No true Montanan really likes the temperature much over fifty, but it has been way over that all month. Today it was eighty-four degrees. I am afraid that global warming, which no doubt started when those Russians put that Sputnik in orbit without asking our permission, is going to plumb ruin the fishing. Trout are a true Montana fish and they don't like it hotter than fifty degrees any more than I do. So they sulk in the shadows and in the deep water, and us guides pay hell trying to get our clients some fish. We have lots of clients, too. Every fishing tourist in America must of heard of Montana, and most of 'em are here. Sometimes we take out two groups a day. They're all excited and sure they are God's gift to fishing and expect to catch a trout every cast even if it is a hundred degrees in the shade.

Elliott says we're jumping around like a one-legged man in an ass-kicking contest, but Elliott isn't writing a bible for young fishermen, so he can say things like that. Actually, that's about the nicest thing he's said lately. He's had his nose in a snit ever since the Fourth of July, and if he doesn't stop being so crabby I'll have to pound some sense into him.

Your July newsletter came the other day. Now, maybe I've just been hanging out in the sun too long with Elliott, but I have a fish bone or two to pick with you guys. First off, I think you ought to elect a new editor. Just because a man is editor of a club newsletter doesn't mean that he has to print every bit of drivel that finds its way to his desk.

I am talking about those five letters to the editor by women saying things like, "Way to go, Beth," and "Show those boys how, Nancy." One woman even listed the names of ten women who were willing to bet a hundred dollars each that Beth and Nance would outfish me and Elliott. Well, all I can say is that the men of New York don't have a very good rein on their wives and girlfriends if they let them throw good money around like that. Rest easy, though; Elliott and me are gentlemen and we wouldn't take advantage of these unguided women. Besides, we are just as busy as I predicted, so that fishing contest will never happen in a million years. I wouldn't of even told my old lady about those articles but Elliott, being some kind of fool, showed a copy to Beth, and now it's all those two women ever want to talk about. Your editor has made my life even more miserable than this heat wave the Russians damned us with.

I hate to be the one who has to point out so many problems with your newsletter, but someone has to do it. I can't believe you published that article by that jerk who claims to have been in Montana, and offered up guesses as to the actual names of the rivers that I have so cleverly disguised. When Hank saw that he said, "What do you have to say to that, Number Three?"

Well, all I have to say to that is, "Wrong, wrong, wrong!" And the only answer any of you guessers will ever get from Donnie Phillips will be wrong.

There was also that short letter titled "A Note to Number III." First off, even though I understand some Latin, I am a true blue Montanan and not descended from Rome. The name is Number Three, not Number III.

Anyway, this letter was directly to me from a guy who just signed his note "Art Curator" over the name of some museum. He asked if I would send him some pictures of my bird carvings. Well, that surprised me; why would anyone want pictures of a guy's whittlings? But I sure guess he can have them if he wants them—Elliott seemed willing to part with them.

He brought them right over and said, "This could be it, Number Three. You're on your way. I bet this guy is real influential in the art world."

"Elliott," I said, "just where do you think I'm going, besides fishing on the Lewis Spoon tomorrow? The man has to be a fool. Hell, he works in a museum. I was in a museum in Helena once when Nancy and I were visiting her mother. We stayed two hours and I was bored after we saw the arrowhead display, which only took about five minutes. Museums are all right for historians and people who like to live in the past but I don't think it's a good idea for anybody to spend much time in one. Nancy spent almost an hour looking at paintings that were older than

America, but I just couldn't see the point. I like to live in the present."

Anyway, you can tell ol' Art that the pictures are on the way. Elliott even made me send the close-ups of the feathers, which don't even show what kind of bird it is and which I was going to throw away. Toss them, Art! I don't need them. And you can keep those pictures of me holding up those big trout. I threw them in because I don't think it's healthy to sit in a dark, damp museum and whittle all day. Why don't you buy a fly rod and come out here to Montana? We'll show you a real adventure.

The rest of the newsletter was okay. It is hard to believe that your second Manhattan Project has already collected thirty thousand dollars in donations. How much did the first one cost? I was gonna send five dollars but it doesn't sound like you need it. Good luck finding a new editor.

Dear Piscatorial Partners,

It's August first. I had promised to tell you about Elliott's month-long grouch but he has gone and stepped on it for good now and has brung me down to ruin with him, which no doubt does not surprise you none. I'll tell you all about it, even though it is a long story and it pains me something awful.

About a week after the Fourth of July we were all in Trudy's before the sun had been awake long, drinking coffee and waiting for our lucky clients. Elliott came in late, looking like he hadn't gone home at all the night before. He hadn't bothered to shave and, sleeping fast like he must of, he'd probably had a passel of bad dreams. He sat down, nodded at me, then zeroed in on Hank. Hank wasn't doing nothing—just minding his own business and eating his breakfast. Like I told you, Hank doesn't eat bacon or eggs or stuff like that. He doesn't even drink coffee, which doesn't have any meat in it. So he was just having his usual, some of Trudy's oatmeal and an English muffin.

Elliott sat down right across from him and stared at that oatmeal like it might be poison. He ordered brown trout and eggs knowing full well that Trudy would never serve such a thing for breakfast. Hank looked at him long and hard but didn't say anything, so Elliott changed his order to steak and eggs, rare and over easy.

Hank got up to change tables but Elliott had to go and make some crack about a man needing his protein if he was going to take care of a real woman. Hank stopped and doubled up his fists and Elliott was standing in a heartbeat, ready for a brawl. I didn't know what the hell was going on. I was getting ready to get between them when Wally walked in with our clients. Hank turned away from Elliott and walked towards Wally. I got up and followed Hank. Elliott sat down to his breakfast and plumb ignored everybody. Wally looked like his mustache had a mouse in it, his face got to twitching so bad. He stared at Elliott's back for a long time. Nothing else happened, though, and we eventually went fishing.

The clients were okay.

Hank got the best two, as usual, a doctor and his wife who have been out here before and are known to be good tippers. And Elliott got the girl—a brunette in her early twenties who was willing to pay extra to be alone with a guide and to get casting lessons. I was just as glad Elliott got her; I ain't no ladies' man. I drew a guy from Seattle named John, and George from Spokane. They didn't know each other, even though they are both from Washington, but they seemed to get along all right and they could both fish a little, too.

We let Elliott and Jane go first so they could get a ways downriver, then stop to practice casting. I didn't think this was fair and said so, but Hank gave me a look worse'n Wally's, and my boat was third again.

It was hard to stay mad, though. It was a great early-summer day with a few clouds and not too damned hot.

The Daffodil was showing off with banks full of daisies. We saw two deer and three ospreys in the first mile of river. My clients spent too much time oohing and aahing over these things, but fish were rising to a Stimulator and they both caught some good trout. A Stimulator is really just a small stone fly pattern with a little orange fluff on it. Hank says the orange is what stimulates the fish to strike, but I think a plain old stone fly would work just as well. Trout seem to be stimulated most of the time anyway. Maybe they are all named Elliott.

Speaking of Elliott, when we went by him he was standing in the water with his arm around Jane and saying ten o'clock and two o'clock as she waved that fly rod back and forth like she had no intention of ever letting the fly land on the water. I could see they had tied on a Stimulator. It was the silliest thing I've ever seen. I've taught a lot of guys how to cast a fly rod and I never put my arms around none of 'em. Hank yelled back at Elliott to catch up by noon and we floated right on by with neither one of 'em hardly glancing up at us.

We kept catching fish, and seeing birds and such—even a pileated woodpecker, which I'll no doubt whittle next—and it would of been a perfect day if we had never stopped for lunch. But, of course, we did.

We had been stopped for most of an hour already before Elliott caught up to us. Our clients had finished their lunches and the doctor and John were wading the river casting for trout. Everybody was anxious to get back on the river; Hank was starting to badmouth Elliott in front of the clients and I thought I was gonna have to bust him one. But Elliott finally showed up. Hank and I ran down to the river and helped him pull the raft up on the bank. Hank started in sputtering at Elliott for being late, but Elliott just ignored him and stepped out of the raft holding a rainbow trout that was a good sixteen or eighteen inches long and was as dead as the tuna in the sandwich I had just eaten.

Now, like I told you before, catch-and-release fishing is the order of the day at the Barbless, and Hank, being a vegetarian and scared to death of dead meat, began yelling at Elliott, asking him stupid questions like who the hell did he think he was, and what the hell did he think he was doing. My clients started moving toward the boat and the doctor and his wife started walking away. I thought I better stick around to protect Elliott, but he didn't act like he needed any help. He just said, "I'm Jane's guide, and this is her first trout, and she wants to eat it. Catch-and-release is a good idea but it's not a religion."

He was standing toe to toe with Hank with his fists all balled up, looking as if he'd like nothing better than a fight. Hank looked ready, too.

I was about to step between them when Jane came up and took Elliott by the arm. She didn't seem to care what Hank thought either. She was carrying a grill and a bottle of wine from the raft and she just said, "Come on,

Elliott, let's eat. I'm starved." She was smiling like maybe she killed something every day.

I thought Hank would lose it for sure. He was all red in the face except where his sunglasses were. He took off his yellow hat and ran his hand through his red hair. He shook the hat at Elliott but finally he put it back on and started walking toward his boat. He growled that Wally was gonna hear about this, and then he got his clients and headed down the river. I could see that Elliott didn't need any more help, so I did the same. By the time we reached the first bend I could see Elliott had a fire going, and I could hear that girl laughing like there was no tomorrow.

DEAR PISCATORIAL PARTNERS,

Back at the shop Wally started in yelling at Elliott, saying stuff like he wouldn't have a surly S.O.B. and a womanizer on his crew and that we by God didn't kill any fish when we were guiding for the Barbless, but Elliott just walked out the door and left Wally there with his mustache twitching.

Wally twitched quite a bit the next two weeks. Elliott kept baiting Hank with all kinds of cracks about his being a vegetarian with a sweet tooth. I didn't understand it, but when I asked Elliott what the hell was going on he just said, "Oh, for Christ's sake, Number Three, don't you have any eyes in your head?"

I could see he was hardly saying anything to his clients, and his boat wasn't landing half the fish the rest of us were catching. He only talked a little to me, which was more than he said to anybody else.

As you have no doubt gathered by now, nothing is sacred to Elliott. He has no respect for anything or anyone. I can tell you that because I already told ol' Elliott the same thing—right to his face, too. We were sitting in the Muddler having a cold beer when Hank walked in and sat down at the other end of the bar. Elliott couldn't leave well enough alone. He ordered a Bloody Mary with a sprig of celery and had Murph deliver it to Hank with a pickled pig's foot. I thought it was a nasty thing to do even though I don't care a damn for Hank. I said, "Elliott, your biggest problem is that you are totally irrelevant."

But Elliott was in no mood for intelligent conversation. He just walked away from me and started in again on Hank. "Say, Hank, I'm cooking trout tonight, why don't you bring your new girlfriend over for dinner?"

Hank just got up and walked out of there, leaving his drink untouched. I said, "I didn't know Hank had a girlfriend."

Elliott never even answered me. He just left me sitting there and went home or someplace. I had one more beer, so Murph wouldn't feel deserted, and went on home myself.

WHEN YOUR BARTENDER IS YOUR ONLY FRIEND, IT IS TIME TO GO HOME.

Beth was there with Nancy. I was beginning to expect that. I hadn't seen Beth with Elliott since the Fourth of July, but I hadn't hardly seen Nance without her. They had two fly rods out in the yard and were practicing. Just as I walked into view Nancy made what must of been a sixty-foot cast. Not too shabby, I thought. I said, "Hi, what's for dinner?"

"Why don't you take us both out?"

Beth has put some strange thoughts in my old lady's head. "Sure, I'll just pull fifty bucks off that money tree I planted last spring."

"Oh, take us out for pizza, silly man. It won't break you."

"Well, I don't know. If you two are serious about this bed-and-breakfast idea, you better practice your cooking."

"We're practicing our casting. Maybe we'll make you the head cook."

I didn't say nothing to that. Hell, I like pizza as well as the next guy. We had just ordered our second pitcher of Pabst Blue Ribbon—even women drink beer with pizza—when I made the mistake of mentioning Hank. "I hear Hank has a girlfriend," was all I said.

Well, Beth turned on me quicker than a rattlesnake in August. "If you mean me, Number Three, I am not his girlfriend. Hank and I have just been out a couple of times, that's all."

"Well, I'll be damned. So that's what Elliott is all in a fuss about."

"I find that hard to believe."

"You'll believe it when you see Hank with two black eyes and his kisser all swelled up. I'm surprised it hasn't happened already."

"Donnie Phillips," said Nancy, "don't be stirring up trouble. It's none of your business."

Well, I guess it is my business if my best friend is being two-timed by a woman he doesn't even go with anymore. I didn't say anything else, though, until Beth had left for home and the old lady and I were having one last beer.

"You know, Nance, I don't understand those two. If Elliott already has a wife, what the hell is he seeing Beth for? And if Beth isn't interested in him anymore, I don't see what difference it makes who she goes out with—though I could fix her up with about a dozen guys better than Hank."

"I think Hank is just a diversion, Donnie."

"Well, I think so, too, but damnit, I wish you wouldn't talk like that in public. You probably ought to tell Beth what you think, though, before she gets any more serious about the guy."

"Oh, Donnie! It's going to be a long life."

And after that we went home and I didn't even think about Beth or Elliott until the next day.

Dear Piscatorial Partners,

Have you ever laughed even though you did not know why?

We met at the shop early the next morning, skipping breakfast at Trudy's because we had a big bunch of clients and we were going quite a ways down the Lewis Spoon to float some water we hadn't fished in quite a while. Elliott walked in right behind me and growled at me, first thing. "Well, Number Three," he said, "I guess you had a good time shooting off your mouth last night."

Well, I would of busted him right there except the phone in the shop was ringing. You see, just about every time the phone has rung lately it's been for Elliott, and it's been the wife he is separated from because he left her in New York. It doesn't take a genius to figure out that she is not happy.

We all try not to listen, even Hank, but when words like "divorce" and "money" get said again and again in a conversation it's not hard to get the digest of what's going on. This day it was even worse.

We all heard Elliott say, "Tommy, watch your mouth! I am still your father." Then he said, "Tommy? Tommy?" and looked at the phone like it had bit him. He hung up slowly, looking pale, his lips closed in a tight thin line.

So Wally right away asked him if he wanted the day off. Elliott said no, but offering was okay of Wally, as it was one of our busiest days. Even Wally was gonna guide two of the four guys that Mr. Italy had sent out from New Jersey. Hank had two guys from Palm Springs he had guided before, so Wally gave Elliott the other two friends of Mr. Italy.

The two guys Elliott would guide were big fellows. I was just as glad I wouldn't have to row them all day. They were maybe in their early fifties, and neither one of them looked to be in very good shape. The bigger of the two was wearing this crazy yellow short-sleeved Hawaiian shirt and a big straw hat. He shook Elliott's hand and said, "Elliott, huh? That's a funny name for a fishing guide. You better be good. We're used to catching a lot of big fish."

Well, I couldn't see what Elliott's name had to do with his skills as a guide, and I might of told this overfed jerk something about that. But as I already pointed out, Elliott has no respect for nobody, so he doesn't need no help holding his own in the mouth department. He growled, "If you fish as good as you talk, we'll do okay."

It was going to be a long day. Wally, who was supposed to be introducing me to my clients, hustled away to grab Elliott by the arm and steer him into the office. All I heard him say before he closed the door was, "For Christ's sake, Elliott." Then I turned toward my clients.

I drew this young married couple from Seattle. They were the first black clients I ever had. The guy shook my hand and said, "My name is David and this is my wife, Linda. What should we call you?"

I don't know why, but I told them they ought to call me Number Three. "You might just as well," I said. "Everybody else does."

Wally had already decided on the order of rafts on the river so I couldn't pass Hank at the last minute and get our raft on the river first. Hank would lead and find the lunch spot. My raft would be next, then Elliott's. Wally would row the last raft.

David and Linda both had some experience fishing. David was the better caster, so he took the stern seat and let his wife sit in the bow of the raft. Both of 'em were willing for me to give some advice, so they each caught a good fish in the first half hour. They were the kind of people you like to guide. They laughed a lot. When David accidentally hung his fly up in some brush on the bank, Linda teased him: "Do you want the bow seat now, honey? I don't seem to be hooking anything but trout up here." I laughed along with them, and rowed to shore so David could save his fly.

Before we could shove off again Elliott's raft passed us. I was surprised he was so close behind us until I noticed that he was hardly rowing at all. The client with the loud shirt and the big mouth was in the bow. He couldn't cast twenty feet, and his friend in the stern wasn't much better. I could hear the Hawaiian fellow jabbering about how he couldn't believe they hadn't caught a single damned fish yet, and how Elliott had better get them into some trout damned soon or he would, by God, be washing dishes in some café instead of guiding for the Barbless. Elliott didn't say a word but, as I mentioned, he had pretty much stopped rowing entirely.

Now, our number one job as guides is to row our rafts upstream against the current. We don't go upstream, of course, but we try to keep the raft floating at about half the speed of the current. That allows our clients time to cast to good water and to get long drifts with their dry flies. It's the work of the job, but it also pays off in numbers of fish caught, which is what makes our clients happy. Elliott's clients weren't about to be happy, so I guess Elliott had decided not to work very hard.

Out of sight, out of mind is what they say, but it was easy to forget about Elliott and his Hawaiian with David and Linda for clients. I was having more fun than I've had all season. Linda hooked a nice rainbow five minutes later and it jumped half a dozen times before she got it close enough to the raft so that I could net it. After I did, David took two or three pictures of me and Linda holding up that fish. He promised to send me one. A few minutes later Linda caught another good fish, and we did the picture thing all over again.

After a while Linda quit fishing. That bothered me some, but she just laughed and said, "Number Three, I'm a bird-watcher, so I'll just spend some time with my binoculars and give David a chance to catch a fish or two." She spotted a scarlet tanager and I had to pull off the river so we could all look at it. It is such a beautiful bird I wished

I could of set right down and whittled one. I will, first chance I get.

David caught two nice trout in the next hour; then we spotted Hank's and Elliott's rafts pulled up on the bank, so we stopped for lunch. Wally came in about ten minutes behind us. Hank's clients were having almost as good a day as David and Linda, but Wally and Elliott were having a guide's nightmare. They had clients who couldn't catch fish in a fish market but who thought they were God's greatest fishermen. Wally had managed to get his guys into three fish, but Elliott's boat had been skunked so far. His clients, of course, blamed him. Elliott wouldn't even talk to them. Mr. Hawaii kept demanding a different guide, and maybe Wally should of give him Hank or something, but he wouldn't. He just suggested that Elliott take over as lead boat with me next, then Wally, and Hank taking up the rear. He also got Elliott aside and jabbered at him some, but I didn't pay much attention as Linda had spotted a bald eagle with her binoculars and the three of us were taking turns looking at it. I should maybe of been talking to Elliott myself, but hind-end sight is always better than forehead sight.

Elliott pushed off and right away Mr. Hawaii hooked himself in the back of his shirt by hurrying his backcast. A cast with a fly rod is really two casts—one backward and one forward—and they should take the same amount of time. If you hurry your backcast, you won't have a good tight loop to cast forward and only God knows where your fly will land. This one ended up right in that fancy yellow shirt. Elliott had to hold his oars with one hand and unhook the fly with the other. Mr. Hawaii started growling about how it wouldn't of happened if Elliott could row a straight course. Elliott just reached out with a pair of scissors he likes to carry in that overloaded vest of his and cut about a two-inch square out of the man's shirt. "There," he said. "Now you can unhook yourself while I practice rowing a straight course."

I started to laugh and so did my clients, but Wally gave me the look so I shut up. David and Linda were still laughing, though, as we shoved off and started fishing. Here is another good rule to put in your notebook:

LAUGHING IS A GOOD THING TO DO ON YOUR FISHING TRIP.

It reminds you why you are here.

And it might of been because we were laughing and having such a good time that we were being so lucky. We could still hear Mr. Hawaii threatening Elliott with how much that shirt was going to cost when Linda hooked another big rainbow. The trout jumped four or five times and both David and I were whooping to make sure everybody saw the fish. Mr. Hawaii had a loud mouth as well as a big one. He said, loud enough for everyone to hear, "Jesus Christ! That tears it. Even that black . . . is catching fish."

I have used a writer's trick of putting three dots in

the sentence because I won't tell you what this fool called Linda. You'll just have to use your imagination; if your imagination does not include such words, you are better off. Linda looked at the clown in the Hawaiian shirt, instead of at her fish, so the line went slack and the trout got off. David looked toward the other boat, too, and got tight lipped. I started rowing down towards Elliott's raft. I guess I was gonna knock that jerk into the middle of next week, but Linda just reached out and touched my arm. "Let it go, Number Three," she said. "Let's just keep fishing."

We did. And we even caught a few more fish. David and Linda even tried to laugh a bit, but it wasn't the same after that. We pulled off the river about five o'clock. We hauled in right next to Elliott's raft, and right away David and Linda started helping pack gear to shore. Elliott's clients weren't helping him a bit. They were just standing near the rafts, drinking beer, and Mr. Hawaii was still at it: "You're gonna get a bill for this shirt in the morning, asshole," he said to Elliott. "And you're through working on these rivers."

Elliott never even looked at him, but David looked over at this big dummy and said, "Why don't you lighten up a little. You're ruining a fine day."

I'll be damned if the other guy from New Jersey didn't mouth off then. He was a big guy, too, but not as fat as Mr. Hawaii. He was wearing clothes from one of those catalogs nobody can really afford and he was smoking a cigar. He was standing right next to me when he decided to open his filthy mouth. He said, "Mind your own business, you effing . . . !" So I pushed him in the river.

I have used three dots again, because the word he called David will never appear in an article I write. And if you ever use that word, I hope someone pushes you in the nearest river. And I hope that river is deeper than the Lewis Spoon, where I threw this guy. He didn't drown but his cigar took a beating. He lost his beer, and his fishing vest was unzipped so a lot of fancy fly boxes and stuff started floating down the river. He was getting to his feet and trying to catch some of that gear when I heard Elliott yell, "Gangway!"

I looked up and here came Elliott holding Mr. Hawaii over his head. Elliott is one strong man for a schoolteacher. He had this fool by the belt and the shirt collar, and he ran down to the river and tossed Mr. Hawaii square on his back in about four feet of water. He went right under and that straw hat was ten feet downstream before he spluttered to the surface again. He took a step towards shore like maybe he was thinking of attacking Elliott, but David stepped right up between Elliott and him and said, "Don't even think about it, my man." Linda was standing right beside him.

That's just how we all stood when Wally and his clients pulled their raft in next to ours: us four on the bank with our fists all balled up, and those two idiots in the water trying to catch a couple hundred dollars' worth of gear they didn't know how to use.

The yelling and screaming sure started then, but Elliott and I ignored them all and just packed up our gear, though we were watching our backs all the time. Wally was so mad he couldn't keep his mustache still, and even Linda started laughing once and said, under her breath, "He looks just like an old walrus."

Mr. Hawaii was telling Elliott and me that we would hear from his lawyer damned soon when Wally got him into his truck along with all the other New Jersey guys and whisked him away. Hank took his clients off, too. So me and Elliott and Linda and David just finished up with the gear. Then we went to the Muddler and had a hard-earned beer. David gave me the biggest tip of the season, even bigger than the one Elliott gave me way back in May, and he gave me his card. "If those guys harass you, call me," he said. "I'm a good lawyer if I do say so myself."

Anyway, we had two beers each; then David and Linda left and Elliott and I went over to the Barbless to put our gear away and to let Wally fire us. He did. And he had a lot to say about it, but Elliott just started in singing, "Jimmy crack corn and I don't care," so I joined in. Wally stormed out of the place and Elliott and I finished with the gear and went on home. We were laughing. I think it's okay.

DEAR PISCATORIAL PARTNERS,

When you're supposed to be the breadwinner and the protector of the female in your family it's not easy to admit that you've been fired. So we just had dinner, and I told Nancy about David and Linda and the trout we caught, and about the big tip I got. But I didn't mention anything about Elliott or Mr. Hawaii or getting canned. Everything in its own time, I figured.

Only timing is not a thing that a man can control, especially when there are women around. At about ten o'clock that night Beth called, and she and Nancy talked for a long time with Nance casting glances my way and raising her eyebrows about every five minutes or so. Finally she called me over and said that Beth wanted to talk to me. She handed me the phone and sat next to me to listen. We aren't one of those American families that think they have to have a phone in every room. We have one, and it's black with a dial, and it sits on a shelf in the kitchen where it belongs. I would of rather had some privacy but I could see Nancy wasn't leaving. So instead of saying hello I just said, "I guess ol' Elliott has been shooting his mouth off again."

"No," said Beth. "Elliott has not been shooting his mouth off. I haven't seen Elliott. He won't even answer his phone. But I hear you two really made fools out of yourselves today, and I wanted to hear your side of the story."

"Is that damn Hank there? I want to have a word with him."

"Hank isn't here. Tell me what happened, please!"

So I told her. I didn't leave anything out, even though it was hard with Nancy listening in on every word.

While I was talking, though, she put her arm around me and rested her head on my shoulder, so I felt some better. When I got done Beth said, "Hmm, that's not the way I heard it."

"Well, that's the way it happened."

"I believe you, Number Three. And I think you did the right thing, even though you and Elliott could probably both have handled it better."

She told me to write everything down, which is no big deal for an author like myself. And she asked me to have Elliott call her as soon as I saw him.

I haven't seen him, though, in three days. I spent those days writing what you've just read and whittling a scarlet tanager. It's coming along fine, and when it's finished I have half a mind to send it to Linda. I think I will.

This morning I got a letter from Wally. It was official notice that I am forever fired from the Barbless. Wally said Mr. Italy had called and said that he never wanted Elliott or me in the shop again, even to buy fly-tying material. He told Wally not to ever buy any more flies from me, either. Wally said that I was lucky, and getting off easy, because he and Hank had taken those two jerks that he called "Elliott's unfortunate clients" on another float, for free, and he had replaced most of the gear they lost, including Mr. Hawaii's shirt. And he was only taking part of that cost out of our last paychecks. He said it was a wonder that I wasn't in jail or getting sued for my last nickel. He said, "I wish you luck, Number Three, but I'll be surprised if you ever get another guiding job in this town."

I thought about taking that letter into the Barbless and jamming it down that fat walrus's throat, but Nancy was home and she just said not to worry. "Things happen for a reason," she said. "This isn't the end of the world."

The funny thing is, I think she's right.

Enclosed in Wally's letter was the August edition of your newsletter. I was really surprised to find out that your editor is a woman and so are your president and vice president. Nancy read that and said she imagined I was embarrassed, having said some of the things I have. But I don't have one embarrassed bone in my body. How was I to know that an editor with the name of Sydney was a woman? I don't know what happened that your editor got named Sydney. I probably don't want to know. I do know that the men of New York must be a bunch of slackers if you have a woman president. You can rest assured that such a thing would never happen in Montana.

I should never of let my old lady read the newsletter. I guess I was concentrating on Wally's letter that made me fired and wasn't paying enough attention. I never even noticed all those letters reserving space for next summer in our bed-and-breakfast, which don't even exist—it is just a filament of my old lady's imagination, so all those women should just forget the whole thing and not get their hopes all in an uproar. Nancy read me the one from Sydney, your female editor, right out loud. I can tell you right now, Sydney, that Beth and Nancy will not be guiding you and your friends on any rivers next summer or ever. And hell will hang thick with icicles before I cook your breakfast.

That letter made me so damned mad I quit whittling and went down to the Muddler, even though I am not presently winning any bread or bringing home the bacon neither, and probably shouldn't be spending money on Pabst Blue Ribbon beer. The Muddler is where I ran into ol' Elliott, and he looked like that's where he has been most of the time since we was fired up at the Barbless.

I asked him if he had got a letter from Wally, making him officially fired. He said he didn't know—that he hadn't checked his mail or answered his phone lately. "No news is good news," he said.

That's a hard point to argue, so I just asked him what he thought he was doing spending so much time at the Muddler. He said, "I'm drowning my sorrows, Number Three."

I read once where some famous writer wrote that sorrows have more lives than cats and I don't find that hard to believe. Anyone who has ever tried to drown a burlap bag full of unwanted kittens in their bathtub knows full well that it's a lot easier to let them grow up to be run over by cars. The same is true of sorrows. They will float right up to the top of a mug of Pabst Blue Ribbon, even if you're drinking the stuff by the pitcher.

I told Elliott all that, but he didn't seem to be listening. He didn't look like the Elliott I was used to seeing. Some men was born to be drunks, but those who aren't should never try to fake it. They'll feel like hell in just a few days and they'll look even worse. I think it's because of the timing. You have to pace your drinking if you're going to be real serious about it, just like you have to time your backcast if you're going to be a serious fisherman. Two of Murphy's regular drunks were sitting up at the bar sipping a whiskey with a beer back, and if you were looking for someone to take to breakfast, you'd of chose either one of 'em over ol' Elliott. He was looking that bad. I figured I better get him out of there.

"Come on, Elliott," I said, "let's go fishing."

"Number Three, going fishing is not God's answer to everything."

IF GOING FISHING IS NOT GOD'S ANSWER TO EVERYTHING, I HAVE NOT HEARD ALL THE QUESTIONS.

I have written that in caps so that you can write it in your notebook, but I also said it to Elliott. He just smiled a bit and said, "You haven't heard all mine, Number Three."

I have heard more than he likes to think but I didn't argue with him. I just said, "Come on, Elliott, I'll take you up to my secret place."

Elliott looked at me kind of surprised, but he was no more shocked than I was. I don't know what got into me. Nancy is the only person I've ever taken up to my place, and I only did that to propose to her. I blindfolded her on the way up, and would of blindfolded her on the way back if she'd of said no.

But Elliott refused me. "I'm probably safer right here at the moment, Number Three. But thank you very much. You are a true friend."

Well, I don't know about that. A true friend would probably of drug him out of there. I was at a loss for words, which is a terrible thing for a writer to admit, and I had lost my thirst just looking at Elliott. I was about to leave him and go on home to whittle when in walked Beth.

She was all dressed up in a gray suit and was wearing this really expensive-looking white hat and carrying a briefcase made from real leather. Dressed that way in the Muddler she stood out like a turd in a bowl of milk.

"Straight from the courtroom to the barroom," muttered Elliott.

"Ah," said Beth, "must be the Lonely Hearts Club. What brings you here, Number Three?"

"I was looking for Elliott."

"Well, you found him. I found him yesterday—same place, same time. Today I was looking for you."

"Why? Is Mr. Hawaii suing us after all?"

"No, you guys lucked out on that one. Actually, I want to talk about the bed-and-breakfast."

"I guess I'll move up to the bar," said Elliott.

"Suit yourself," Beth said. Then she ignored him and opened that fancy briefcase. Elliott stayed where he was. The first thing she pulled out was a copy of the New York newsletter edited by that woman named Sydney. "Have you seen this?" she asked me.

"Enough of it. That fool woman edits out about every other word I say."

"I mean all those letters requesting reservations at our fishing lodge."

"They're just a bunch of crazy women having pipe dreams about how to spend their poor husbands' money."

"Number Three, don't be a fool. We're sitting on a gold mine here."

"I know it," I said, "but Murph already owns it, and he'll throw us out soon if we don't order a drink."

Elliott laughed, signaled Murph for three drinks, and picked up the newsletter, which was laying untouched in front of me.

"Damnit," said Beth. "This is our big chance. I don't believe you're willing to pass it up. It's time for you to look at your future." She looked at me, bit her lip, and added, "You owe it to Nancy." She didn't even glance at Elliott, who was paying Murph for two beers and one gin and tonic.

I'm more interested in taking big fish than big chances and I don't need no woman lawyer to tell me my responsibilities and I told her so. "Why are you so hot to change my life?" I asked her. "Why do you care what I build on my father's land? Who gives you the right to put all these ideas in my wife's head? And what makes you think I want her to become a fishing guide?"

"He's got a point," butted in Elliott.

"Who the hell asked you?" we both said at once.

Elliott laughed again. "You're sitting at my God-damn table. Just ask Murph. I've been parked in the same place for most of the past three days. Say, Number Three," he went on, like Beth and me weren't in the middle of an important disagreement, "did you read this newsletter?"

"Some of it," I said. "I read all my stuff—what little that female editor included—I pretty much quit reading all those lies those other people write about fishing all over the damned world."

"Well, I think you better read this!"

Elliott handed me the newsletter, pointing to the article he wanted me to read.

"Can't this wait? We were in the middle of an important discussion."

"No, Beth," said Elliott, "it can't wait. Besides, you ought to think about what Number Three is saying. You and Nancy aren't considering him in your plans. You don't want to wreck their marriage, do you?"

"You are a fine one to talk about wrecking marriages."

"I am the perfect one to talk about it. I am quite good at it."

"I'm sorry, Elliott, I didn't mean that."

"It's okay, but why don't you go for a walk with me? We'll let Number Three read his article. You can talk to him some more later."

Then they up and left. I drank my beer while I read the piece in the newsletter. It wasn't really an article. It was titled "A Note to Number III" and it was another letter from Art, who works in that museum in New York City. It was short, so I'll just put it right in here. It has already been in the newsletter but Sydney will cut it out anyway. She is a ruthless woman.

> *Dear Number III,*
>
> *Thank you for sending the pictures. I was quite impressed. You have the skilled hand and imaginative eye of a true artist. Please send me two or three of your carved birds. I would like to consider your work for an extensive showing. All work sent will be returned and insured.*

Well, I guessed I could send a couple of birds to this guy, if Nancy didn't mind. I couldn't see much point in it, though. What kind of man would hang around an old museum and get all excited about a little whittling that another guy does just to pass the time when there's no fishing to be done? I was damned sure I never wanted to meet Art Curator. I couldn't understand Elliott's excitement, neither, but I was awful glad that he had gotten Beth out of my hair.

DEAR PISCATORIAL PARTNERS,

Beth is not really out of my hair. She and Nancy spent most of last evening walking around our place talking about how they would set up the bed-and-breakfast and where they would build a shed for half a dozen rafts and stuff. I let them dream. They were having gin and tonics and were giggling so I didn't want to drown them in the cold water of reality. Reality is that I will not allow them to build this place and I will never work for no woman outfitter.

They wanted to drag me along but I had work to do. I had to select some birds to send to Art. Nancy was even more thrilled than Elliott when I showed her the note in the newsletter. I don't understand why she's so excited unless it's just her natural female instinct to take care of misguided ragamuffins that can't do no better than work in a museum.

Nancy even took all the birds out of the house and dusted them and put them in the shop. The first thing I did was to count them. I have whittled fifty-seven birds. That may not seem like a lot, since I already told you I've been whittling since I was a little boy, but I didn't start right in whittling birds. I started in with pointed sticks and worked my way up to birds. I see them when I'm out hiking or at work on the river, and then I come home and look them up in my old lady's bird book. I use the book for detail and size and color (sometimes I paint my birds, but not always), but I whittle them from the memory of how I saw them in the wild.

A HOBBY IS A GOOD THING TO HAVE, BECAUSE IT KEEPS A MAN FROM ALWAYS WISHING HE WAS FISHING.

That's a good thing to remember. My hobby is saving me right now since Mr. Italy has banished me from the Barbless. "Banished" was the word Elliott used when we were in the Muddler. "Number Three," he said, "we are banished. Banished from the Barbless, by some rich despot sitting on his throne in New Jersey. We must not succumb to this treachery. We shall overcome!"

We'd had a couple of Pabst Blue Ribbons by the time Elliott got around to spitting out that mouthful, so I didn't even try to figure out what it all meant or if it was all in English or not. I started laughing, though, because in my house the throne is the toilet. I could just see this fat little guy sitting on his toilet, using dollar bills for toilet paper and waving a cigar in the air, declaring Elliott Prince and Donnie Phillips forever banished from the Barbless Connection.

So I was glad I had my hobby. I packed up the pileated woodpecker that I just finished a while back. I also sent Art a ruffed grouse I carved a long time ago, and a chickadee, which might be my favorite bird, cause it will fly right up next to you when you're in the pines in the winter and tell you its name. Then I painted the last coat of paint on the scarlet tanager. When it's dry I'll send it to Linda and David.

I had just finished painting the tanager when Beth and Nancy burst into the shop. They were laughing and holding hands. I'll have to talk to Nancy about that kind of behavior, even though I know that Beth is the weird one of the two. Anyway, they came in and Beth started looking at all the birds I had whittled. She kept picking them up and running her fingers over them. "Number Three," she said, "you are amazing. I had no idea."

Ain't it just like a woman to go crazy over a little whittling? I was foolish, though. I let my guard down. Before I knew it I was telling Beth all about the birds I had seen, and why I tried to whittle them just like I saw them. She kept nodding and acting excited, and then she just dropped a bomb on me. She said, "What kind of birds do you think we'll see on our fishing trip, Number Three?"

"It's hard to tell. Wait a minute! What fishing trip?"

"The one you and Elliott promised you'd take Nancy and me on when you weren't busy guiding. You certainly aren't busy, and it would be good to drag Elliott out of the Muddler. Besides, it's a contest, and you promised that if Nancy and I won we could start work on the bed-and-breakfast. You get to pick the river—remember?"

I didn't remember any such thing and I told her so. I kept telling Nancy the same thing for so long after Beth left that I wound up sleeping on the couch. She says I can sleep there until we go on our fishing trip. Women never fight fair.

DEAR PISCATORIAL PARTNERS,

I think I was too generous, sending Art three birds. It cost me over twenty dollars at the post office, and now I'm worried that a guy who has to work in a museum won't have enough cash to send them back. I mailed the tanager to Linda, too, so I just had barely enough money left for a couple of beers at the Muddler. I had to go, though. I needed to find Elliott. I had a plan.

Elliott was not in the Muddler even though it was well after ten A.M. when I got there. I ordered a beer from Murph and decided to wait for Elliott. It irked me, though, his being so late. It's what I mean when I say Elliott is not cut out to be a serious drunk. A real drunk would be hard at work on his favorite bar stool long before ten in the morning. Elliott has no self-respect, which is why he has no respect for anybody else. If he just did everything he did good, we wouldn't both be out of work and I wouldn't have to come up with a plan to scare my old lady away from the dangerous business of becoming a fishing guide.

I had it all figured out, though. There's a river a few hours away from town where we guides sometimes take special clients in the fall of the year. I won't tell you the real name of it, but I'll tell you that it is one of the many Montana rivers named after one of our great presidents. It isn't the Richard Nixon River; we haven't discovered that river yet, though I'm sure we will. I'll call it the Milhous River to further confuse those New Yorkers who are spending every waking moment trying to guess what rivers I'm writing about.

The Milhous is a good September fishery for brown trout, but it is treacherous because of all the divergent dams on it. Divergent dams are almost as nasty as they sound. They are dams built by ranchers to change the direction of the river water from where it wants to go to the fields where the rancher wants to grow hay for his cattle. They let the water go back in the river before it reaches their neighbor's land. So the neighbor has to build a divergent dam himself, which means the damn things are spread all up and down the Milhous River, about every six miles or so, which is how much land a Montana rancher likes to own for starters. Most ranchers have never worked for the U.S. Army Corps of Engineers, and if they have gone to college at all they've mostly studied fertilizer spreading and weight lifting, so their dams are not works of art like the Corps makes. Some ranchers are so rich that they have their own bulldozers, but most of 'em just push rocks or refrigerators or old cars into the river to make their dams.

Rowing over divergent dams is not for the timid. It pained me to do it, but my plan was to send Beth and my sweet wife over one of these dangerous dams. Elliott and I would save them, of course, and then we could come on home and that would be the last ever heard of this fool bed-and-breakfast idea.

I couldn't wait to tell Elliott my plan, but I'd already drunk three beers and he still hadn't showed up. I was, in fact, the only one in the Muddler besides Murphy's two regulars, even though it was by now way past eleven. I'd just spent the last of my cash on a fourth Pabst Blue Ribbon when somebody finally walked through the Muddler's swinging door. I turned around to greet Elliott, but I was instead looking straight at Hank, who started to grin.

"Well, well, if it isn't Number Three, fishing the tepid waters flowing from Mahogany Ridge."

"What the hell are you doing here? Did Mr. Italy banish you, too?"

"Not in your wildest dreams, Number Three. I just needed a day off to count my money. It has been a good year."

"Well, why don't you count it somewhere else. Murph doesn't serve no vegetable burgers in here."

"You talk awful tough for a guy who's going to be working for his old lady. I wonder how long it'll be before she gets smart and fires you."

There are limits to what even a peace-loving guy like myself can take. I jumped to my feet and went over to teach this fool from Venice a lesson.

I don't know how to explain it. All I can figure is that Hank's eyes were still wide open from being out in the sunshine, while mine were closing in the dark of the Muddler. Anyway, he saw my nose more clearly than I could see his fist. It was just dumb luck, but he caught me square on the snot locker and I landed on my back with blood flying everywhere. You know by now that a little blood will not keep Donnie Phillips down. I was about to get up and teach Hank a real lesson when Murphy yanked me to my feet. "You're out of here, Donnie! I don't want to see you for a month. I don't allow any daytime fighting in my bar. It upsets my regulars."

That was a new rule on me. Once more Hank's bacon was saved. I have to say that Murph's regulars didn't look very upset. I'm not even sure they noticed. Now I'm banished from the Barbless and the Muddler and my own damn bed. I can tell you for sure that it is not a fair world. Hank was laughing when I walked out of the Muddler, but he'll get his. I didn't even look for Elliott anymore, just went on home. There was no beer in the fridge.

DEAR PISCATORIAL PARTNERS,

This should be some fishing trip. It's scheduled for September second, which is two weeks from now, and I'll be glad when the damned thing is over and things get back to normal around the Donnie Phillips house. Nancy is only talking to me to say, "Please pass the pepper," or, "Will you pick up some toilet paper today in your free time." She says "free time" like it's my fault I have any. She said she would not stay married to a man who thought having a good time was getting beat up in a beer joint. It didn't help when I explained to her that I did not get beat up, but that Murph invented some fool new rules to protect Hank. When I told her that the Muddler was not a beer joint, she wouldn't even listen to me, but instead went and spent the night at Beth's.

It's the first time that Nancy has threatened to leave me. It makes me think that Beth is looking for divorce court work. I never did believe that she had enough money to start no bed-and-breakfast. Beth isn't talking to Elliott, either. He said that after they left me in the Muddler and took that walk, the air had cleared but the atmosphere was still damned chilly.

At least Elliott and me are talking to each other. He came over the day after I got into it with Hank. He was all cleaned up and shaved. I guess he got smart and gave up his plan to become the town drunk. His first words to me were: "Christ, Number Three, you look like death warmed over."

I changed the subject and told him my plan.

All he said when I was done was, "That's diversion dam, not divergent dam, Number Three, and I doubt that a diversion dam is about to intimidate our gal Beth."

I told him she was not my gal and it didn't look much like she was his either. And that I didn't plan to intimidate her, but rather to scare the living hell out of her.

Elliott flat out told me that it wouldn't work. "I don't even know if I want to go," he said. "I haven't felt much like fishing lately."

That right there is the problem with out-of-staters moving to Montana. They end up living right here in the middle of the best place on God's green earth and they wake up day after day not even wanting to go fishing. People like that just don't belong here.

DEAR PISCATORIAL PARTNERS,

It is now the first of September and I have a crick in my back from sleeping on our damned old couch. If I was working regular I would go out and buy a new one, putting an end to all this nonsense.

The fishing trip is on. Beth came over the other day with the rules and a piece of paper for me to sign saying I agreed to them and to the terms of the wager. Have you ever noticed that lawyers don't trust anybody and never take a man's handshake as gospel? It pains me to think that my old lady is in cahoots with such a woman as Beth. But at least this fishing trip will put an end to all that.

The rules were all typed up on what Beth called legal paper, but I've never seen no illegal paper so I just think she was trying to sound more important than she ever will be. Just look at these damned rules she dreamed up:

RULES OF CONDUCT
FOR THE MILHOUS RIVER REGATTA

1. Team A will consist of Nancy Phillips and Beth Sanders.

2. Team B will consist of Donnie Phillips and Elliott Prince.

3. Teams will depart for the Milhous River at 4 A.M. on September 2 in separate vehicles.

4. Teams may begin fishing as soon as they reach the prearranged put-in.

5. All fishing must be done with fly rods and barbless hooks. No spinning gear allowed.

6. Teams may fish until dark. The official fish counter for team A will be Nancy Phillips. Elliott Prince will count for team B. Fishing will end at dark. The team with the most fish wins. All fish counted must be trout; size is not a consideration.

7. Tallies will be compared at the take-out right after dark.

8. Teams will provide their own tent or tents and food if they plan to camp at the take-out. Members of team A will not sleep with or cook for members of team B.

9. Team members will return on September 3 in their respective vehicles.

10. May the best team win.

I was gonna argue about rule eight but it wasn't really any different from sleeping on the couch. I told Elliott right out he had to bring his own tent. I told Nancy I didn't want her sleeping in the same tent with Beth either but she just said, "Oh, Donnie, don't be ridiculous."

The woman doesn't understand the dangers the world is full of.

The wager was spelled out on the next page. Basically if Elliott and I win, I won't have to hear nothing more about this bed-and-breakfast idea. If Beth and Nancy win (which they have no chance of), we will begin construction immediately, and I'll agree to guide for Beth for one year and to allow Nancy to guide when she wants.

I wanted to include that, if we won, Beth would move out of town and have no further contact with my wife, but neither of them would go along with that because they know they are bound and determined to lose. So I left well enough alone and went ahead and signed. When Elliott saw what I had done he said, "Jesus, Number Three, you've gone and bet the whole farm."

I told him the farm was safe so long as he remembered to think like a trout. He promised to try.

DEAR PISCATORIAL PARTNERS,

Elliott showed up at ten minutes to four just like we planned. Beth had already been there for fifteen minutes and she and Nancy were having breakfast and giggling like they were going to a damned prom or something. Beth kept saying things like, "Don't forget your waders, Number Three."

She was giving me a hard time because I was breaking my own rule and wasn't wearing my waders to breakfast. We had a good three-hour drive ahead of us and I wasn't about to wear my waders for that long. Besides, I wasn't really having breakfast. I just filled two thermoses with coffee while Elliott loaded his gear in the rig. We were ready to leave only five minutes after Beth and Nancy had taken off. I thought my wife would kiss me good-bye. She came over to me like she might, then she just touched my shoulder and almost ran out the door. You'd of thought she was crying or something. I wanted to say good luck, but if she had good luck I'd be ruined. So I didn't say a thing.

Elliott and I didn't say much for the first part of the trip, neither. I concentrated on my driving, figuring I would pass Beth as soon as we got up on the interstate. But Beth has no respect for the amount of America's gas she burns up. I never did catch up with her and I gave up trying soon after Elliott woke up enough to say, "For Christ's sake, Number Three, will you slow down? You're scaring the bejesus out of me."

Sometimes Elliott is the wimp his name suggests, but the trailer holding Ol' Red, my raft, had started to whip back and forth, so I slowed down to sixty-five or so. Besides, I had another plan for passing Beth and having our raft in the water first. Everything in good time; that's what my daddy always said.

Elliott is not a true blue river guide and has not yet learned how to hold his coffee, so we had to stop twice to pee. But even so we made good time to the shortcut. When I made the turn onto this gravel road, Elliott grabbed the map and said, "Number Three, where the hell do you think you're going?"

"Don't you worry your little head, Elliott. It's all a part of my plan."

It was. And it would of worked, too, if it hadn't of been for those sandhill cranes. There were eleven cranes, and two of 'em were right on the road. We were only about a mile from the river by then, me driving as fast as I dared on that bumpy old road, and I just hated to stop. Sandhill cranes are giant birds that God no doubt put on earth to give men the idea that we should invent airplanes. They're not a bird that we see near home. In fact it's only when I get over in the part of the state where the rivers are named after presidents that I ever see sandhill cranes. I'd never seen any up this close so I had to stop. I've never tried to whittle a sandhill crane, but I thought if I could get a good look at one I might be able to. I only figured to stop for a minute but, of course, I forgot about Elliott.

He was out of the car in a heartbeat with that fool camera of his. The birds on the road walked off into the brush and Elliott was right behind them, crawling on his belly. I figured he'd crawl right over a rattlesnake and we'd be in a real fix and lose the contest for sure. But he didn't. Still, it was a good twenty minutes before he came back to the truck. He was all excited, too, said he got some great shots and he'd give me copies to whittle from. I said, "Just get in the rig, will you, before those fool women catch all the fish and my workshop becomes a damned bed-and-breakfast."

He did, and we spun off towards the river, throwing gravel all over Ol' Red. I wasn't really worried, though. You see, I knew something about this put-in on the Milhous River.

The first divergent dam is right there at the put-in. You either have to float right down through it, first thing, or you have to carry your gear and your boat a good hundred yards downstream. Running over the dam is not a problem for an experienced river guide like myself, but it would be a scary deal for a couple of fool women who fancied themselves to be piscatorial experts. Beth and Nance might already be at the put-in, but if they were, they were no doubt busy hauling their gear downstream. They would still be carrying stuff when we floated by them. To top it off there was a big foam pocket, right at the bottom of the dam, where I figured we would catch our first brown trout of the day.

Beth and Nancy were there, but they hadn't carried their boat downstream. They were sitting in it in some quiet water just above the dam, waiting for us, I guess. I jumped out of the truck to tell them they better just unload and start walking, but as soon as my feet hit the ground Beth yelled, "Let the contest begin," and pushed out into the main stream. The current grabbed that blue raft of theirs, Nance gave out a little squeal, and they were flying over the dam. I quick untied my lines and started dragging Ol' Red off the trailer so as we could save them, but Elliott said, "Not to worry, Number Three. They're over it. Well, I'll be damned! Nancy has already hooked a big brown out of that foam pocket. Look at that, Number Three! She's holding it up. We are behind already."

He sounded happy. I said, "Whose damn side are you on, anyway? Let's get a move on here!" I made sure that I didn't look at Nancy holding up her fish except out of the corner of my eye. Elliott finally got his rod put together and we pushed off. Beth and Nancy were long out of sight.

There is a second way over the dam, on the far side of the river. It's trickier, because you can't see over the edge before you go, but there's another good foam pocket over there. We needed a trout to catch up so that's where I headed.

"I don't know about this, Number Three," said Elliott, who is not the bravest friend I've ever had. "I can't see what's over there."

"It's just water, Elliott. Don't worry. Just get ready to drop that Woolly Bugger right in that foam pocket." I pushed off.

We would of been just fine, too, except Elliott yelled "look out!" way too late. There was a broken stump of a cottonwood tree lodged halfway down the dam and by the time Elliott yelled, there was no way I could of missed it, strong as I am. I tried, you can believe that. But the left front of Ol' Red rammed right into the broken point of that damned stump. I told you before that Ol' Red has some age on her. That raft has seen a lot of water and not a few rocks, so she's grown rather thin skinned. That stump blew a hole in her as big as my head.

Now, being from New York and not being used to rafts and such, you might think that it was all up with us and we were pitched into the drink and lucky not to drown. Elliott did, in fact, have to do some fancy scrambling to stay in the raft, and I had all I could do to hang on to the oars and get us free of that snag. But Ol' Red is a good raft and not made all in one section, but rather in six, so only one compartment had exploded and we still were floating high and dry on the other five. I rowed to shore once we got through the dam and we tied up the exploded section, best we could, with duck tape, which Elliott says is really duct tape, even though he hasn't used half as much of it in his life as I have. I say:

YOU CAN CALL IT WHATEVER YOU WANT BUT DUCK TAPE SHOULD ALWAYS BE IN YOUR BOAT, OR IN YOUR VEST, OR SOMEWHERE HANDY. IT CAN FIX ALMOST ANYTHING, EVEN A BROKE LEG.

Anyway, we got Ol' Red floatable again by turning the rowing frame around, making the stern into the bow, which is a great thing about rafts that makes them better than hard boats. You can point them any direction you want, within reason. We had to leave one of our coolers behind to lighten the load, and Elliott chose the one with the Pabst Blue Ribbon, keeping the one with the food. That wouldn't of been my choice but he said, "Number Three, if you jettison my dinner you'll have to go without me," and, as I would have a tough time outfishing those two women without him, I had no choice. I reminded him that we would already be downriver with lunch and beer if he had only yelled sooner. Then I grabbed three beers out of the cooler and let him hide the rest in the brush. "Let's get the hell going," I said.

We had to. We'd been screwing around for most of an hour and the sun was already starting to shine on the water. This did not make me happy. Those women had fished a good hour in the early morning, which we had missed through no fault of my own. It wasn't fair. And now the damned sun was shining. Don't get me wrong, I like the sun as well as the next guy. It is fine on those rare days when all a guy has to do is to lie around and drink beer. But the sun is no friend to the serious trout fisher-man. Brown trout are shy, or maybe their skin is as sensi-tive as a human redhead's. Anyway they like to sulk in the deep water and in the shade on a sunny day. They are much easier to catch when there are some great clouds cumulating up in the sky.

So I knew the fishing would be slow, and it was. It took Elliott most of another hour to catch his first trout even though I was rowing that crippled raft as hard as I could. Half an hour later, with Elliott having only caught one more pitiful small trout, I took over fishing.

I was worried a bit about Elliott rowing that broken raft but he took to it okay, and I started fishing hard. We had to make up for lost time. I fished real deep with slow retrieves I would make by just weaving in the line with short movements of my left hand. It paid off, too. I hadn't even been fishing an hour when I hooked and landed a brown trout twice as big as either one of Elliott's. That made three fish. I started to feel better. Five minutes later I hooked one that I know was even bigger, but Elliott knocked it off when he was trying to net it. "Damnit, Elliott. Are you trying to ruin me?"

"Why Number Three, I thought we were fishing for fun."

Well, that remark made me almost mad enough to throw him into the river. We were fishing for my life and he damn well knew it. I didn't say anything, just started casting. I was too damned mad, though, and not paying attention, so my retrieve was too fast. By the time I remembered, and caught another fish, a half hour had gone by. It was getting late in the morning and we only had four fish. I tried to get Elliott to count the one he had knocked off with the net, but he wouldn't.

We came up to the second divergent dam just before noon. We had switched rowers a couple of times but we hadn't caught any more fish. Elliott was rowing again. "There they are," he said, pointing.

The blue raft was sitting in some quiet water across the river. Nancy was at the oars and Beth was waving at us to come over. Elliott started rowing over to them but I stopped him. "Don't be a fool, Elliott," I said. "This is our chance to get ahead of them for the evening fishing."

"I don't know, Number Three. Beth has a good head on her. She probably stopped for a good reason. This dam looks even trickier than the first one."

"It is trickier, but there's a good route down straight ahead of us. I've done it before. Just change places with me and I'll row us through it, slick as a whistle. It's time to teach these women a thing or two about river rafting."

I reeled in and got ready to take over the rowing but I should of remembered that Elliott has no respect for anybody or anything. "No, Number Three," he said. "You already tried to drown us once. Now it's my turn."

With that he pushed us forward into the grip of the current. Both women were yelling at us now, but there was no turning back, so we just waved and went over the edge of the dam.

This dam is more dangerous than the first one because it's higher and the water moves faster. Halfway down there are some rocks where the oarsman has to row like hell and pull the boat over to the right. After that it's clear sailing. This year, just because my lucky stars haven't been in the sky since Elliott got here, part of a tree was hung up in those rocks. It made the hazard about twice as big as normal, with that log half under the water and stretched out like a poisonous snake. Unlike Elliott I yelled out in plenty of time. I even have to give Elliott credit: He really bent into those oars. I think we would of missed everything, except that damned duck tape must of loosened up when we weren't looking. The deflated part of the raft was dragging in the water and it caught on that damned log.

As soon as it did the raft went sideways in the fastest part of the current. Water started to pour in. I tried to stand up to help unhook us but I was knocked right into the river. I even dropped my fly rod, I was so surprised. Elliott must of been thrown free, too, because we were both in the drink. I heard him yelling behind me as I was being washed down the dam. I saw his head once and the cooler bobbing behind him. I guess we forgot to tie the cooler down when we were rearranging things. Then I was washed under water. I would of been okay. I'm a good swimmer. But I had hit something and my waders were tore and filling up with water. I got my head above water again, once I reached quiet water, but just barely, like one of those old plastic red-and-white bobbers that has a crack in it. I could see, though. I saw Elliott crawling out on the far shore, and then I saw the blue raft coming over the dam. Nancy was rowing, her hair flying out behind her and her arms working like crazy. Beth was in the bow, and she was pointing, and it looked like she was yelling. I slipped under the water again then. I must of hit my right knee on a rock or something, because it hurt awful and I was having trouble kicking with my boots full of water like they were. I got back up long enough to gasp some air, and then I sank again.

The next thing I knew Beth had a hold of my hair and then my arm, and she was yanking me over the side of that raft. She is one strong woman, I can tell you that. I slid into the raft and just lay there catching my breath. Nancy rowed us over to shore. Then she just sat there, and I could see by the way her shoulders were shaking that she was crying. Elliott was walking down the shore so Beth jumped out of the raft and ran towards him.

"You damned fool, Donnie Phillips. You could have drowned."

That was all Nancy said. I didn't have anything to say, so I just rubbed my sore knee and kept my mouth shut.

After a few minutes I got out of the raft and took off my worthless waders. My knee was only bruised but it was already stiffened up, so I limped whenever I tried to walk. The sun was still warm but I was shaking anyway. Nancy dug a blanket out of their dry bag and came over and wrapped it around me. Then she kissed me. I still didn't say anything. The women broke out some lunch and we all had some. Then Beth and Elliott rowed over beneath the dam with a rope and, though I didn't think they had a snowball's chance in the devil's own furnace, they finally got a line on Ol' Red and jerked her loose from that log. There wasn't much left of Red but we saved my rowing frame, our dry bag full of clothes (and Elliott's camera), and our life jackets, which were wedged between the raft frame and the raft. Nancy rolled her eyes when we found them. I noticed that both Beth and Nancy still had their life jackets on. A good rule for you to write down and remember is:

IF YOU WEDGE YOUR LIFE JACKETS WHERE THEY ARE HARD TO GET YOU ARE APT TO LOSE THEM, AND A GOOD LIFE JACKET WILL RUN YOU MOST OF FIFTY DOLLARS.

Elliott dove for our fly rods and got lucky and found both of 'em, if you want to call any part of that day lucky. Finally the four of us piled into that blue raft of Hoolihan's and headed for the take-out. There's a road down to that dam so we left Ol' Red and the rowing frame and the one oar we found on the beach, to pick up on the way home. Beth rowed; nobody fished, and nobody had much to say. When we were nearly to the take-out Beth cleared her throat kinda nervously. "It might be a bad time to ask," she said, "but how many trout did you guys catch?"

I looked hard at Elliott so he would know to count the fish he had made me lose, but he just said, "Four. We just caught four, two each."

Beth was grinning like she'd just caught up to an ambulance. "Looks like we're in business, Nancy."

But Nancy just shook her head. "I'm the official counter for our boat, and I only counted four. I guess it's a tie." Then she turned around and wouldn't talk to any of us. Beth's mouth opened and shut a couple of times, like she was getting ready to argue a murder case, but she didn't say a word. I knew there was a good pocket of foam, just before the take-out, where there was no doubt a big brown. I thought about picking up Nancy's rod and making a couple of casts to break the tie but, for reasons I don't understand, I decided against it.

I had hired a guy from a nearby fly shop to run the shuttle for us, so Beth's car was parked right by the take-out. We loaded the raft on the trailer and then headed back to pick up my truck. We had camping gear in the rigs but we decided that we would drive on home. When we got to my truck, Nancy surprised me. She looked at Elliott and Beth and said, "If it's all the same to you, I would like to ride home with my husband." And that's what she did.

Dear Piscatorial Partners,

I now have a lawyer. It was Nancy's idea. Now, don't go jumping to conclusions on me. I jumped to the same ones you are probably leaping on, but for once I was wrong. You see, Nancy and I started talking almost as soon as we got in the truck and headed home from the Milhous River, and we talked all the way home. I started out by asking her how many fish they really caught. She told me not to ask. "You don't really want to know," she said. "Be happy with the tie, Donnie. We are asking you to change your life. You have to decide. It shouldn't be decided by a silly contest. I think you ought to get a lawyer."

That threw me. "Why do I need a lawyer? Has that woman talked you into leaving me? I . . ."

"Donnie, don't be a fool. I'm not leaving you. I love you. I just want you to take a good look at Beth's ideas for the bed-and-breakfast. Let's have her draw something up. We'll have another lawyer look at it to make sure we can't lose our land or anything. Then we'll talk about it. If you still don't want to do it, we won't."

"Do I still have to sleep on the couch?"

Nancy laughed. "Not tonight, anyway," she said.

So I'm no longer sleeping on the couch, and I have a lawyer. His name is George Adams, and we went to high school together. He usually hires me about once a year to take him and his brother-in-law fishing. He says it's not worth having all the equipment if you only get to fish once or twice a year. It's easier just to hire a guide. I guess that's right, but why would a man want to spend all his days in a courtroom and only fish once or twice a year? I think old George went sour after high school. I know he went out of state somewhere to go to law school. I can't say it did him much good. But he's supposed to be a good lawyer and he's willing to do part of the work in trade for a fishing trip next year. I told him it's a deal, even though I may have to rent a blue raft from Hoolihan. Ol' Red is beyond repair.

Beth told Nancy that she would be glad to write up a formal proposal and to submit it for our scrutiny. I don't know what a bed-and-breakfast has to do with getting married and I am already hitched to Nancy, but I guess I can read it, anyway. My lawyer will probably tell me who it is that Beth's planning to marry.

It won't be Elliott. That's for sure. Elliott called me two days after we got back from the Milhous River and asked me to meet him for a beer at the Muddler. I had to remind him that I was still banished from the Muddler so he said he would bring a six-pack out to the house. "Do you have time to talk, Number Three?"

I have plenty of time; all I seem to be doing lately is whittling. I told him that, so he came on out. He got here right after the mailman. I had just finished reading the letter from David and Linda. They had said to say "hi" to Elliott, so I let him read the letter. It was mostly a thank-you note. I guess Linda really likes the scarlet tanager I whittled for her. She said she's showed it to a whole bunch of their friends and that quite a few of them would be interested in buying some of my birds. She said I should send her a price list if I was interested. "Don't make it cheap, Number Three; these carvings of yours are really fine, and my friends don't mind spending good money for quality art."

Elliott said, "Hmm," and raised his eyebrows when he read that line. "It looks like you're on your way, Number Three. You deserve it, too, you are almighty handy with that whittling knife of yours. And more creative than I ever would've imagined."

I wasn't sure I liked that last statement but I didn't make a ruckus. I just opened one of his beers and said, "I'm not about to sell my birds. I already gave most of 'em to Nancy, anyway. Whittling is just a hobby. What I really need is to find a way to finance a new raft. Next year I have to really get serious about my fishing."

"Maybe it's time to consider some serious changes."

That crack made me mad and I was about to really light into Elliott for butting into my business. When I looked up, though, he was gazing off right over my head and scratching his freshly shaved chin. Honest, I didn't know if he had been talking to me or to himself. So I didn't say nothing.

A MAN HAS TO KNOW WHEN NOTHING IS THE RIGHT THING TO SAY.

Elliott stood there a minute. Then he looked straight at me. "It's time for me to take charge of my life, Number Three. I've decided to go back home to see if I can straighten out my marriage. Maybe there is little to do except get a divorce and go on from there. But at least I'll find out. I'm not accomplishing much right now, that's for sure. Maybe I'll even end up back out here. Who knows?"

Well, it is just not a fair world when a man works his fanny off to make a new friend and that guy up and moves two thousand miles away. I told Elliott that but he just smiled. "Number Three, you ought to be half tickled that I'm leaving. I'm the guy that wrecked your raft, remember? I wish I could afford to buy you a new one, but I can't. I have no idea what's about to happen to my finances. At least," he said with another grin, "I don't have any ideas that sound very good."

"You don't owe me no raft," I said. "Ol' Red was worn out already. We'd of probably been better off renting one of Hooligan's."

"Great idea, Number Three. He'd be howling now, wouldn't he?" Elliott was laughing right out loud.

"Howling Hooligan," I said and we were both about rolling on the floor. When I stopped laughing, Elliott handed me another beer.

"So I guess this is good-bye for now, Number Three."

"When are you leaving?"

"Tomorrow morning."

"Tomorrow morning? Boy, you don't waste any time, do you?"

"I figure I've wasted enough already."

After that we didn't say much for a while, just drank our beers. Elliott was looking off over my head again so I started thumbing through the rest of my mail. There was a big official envelope from that museum in New York City where Art lives, so I opened that next.

The first page was just a short typewritten note. Art is not a man of many words. He just said, "It is my pleasure to offer you a one-man showing in the nature room of our museum, January 15 through January 30. Opening will be on January 15. We will pay airfare for you, plus shipping charges for your art, plus three days' lodging in the city. All other expenses are your responsibility. A standard contract is enclosed. Please reply before October 15."

I showed Elliott the note and he said, "My oh my, Number Three. You're headed for the big time now. This is serious stuff."

I thought I'd cured Elliott of saying "my oh my," but I guess some things never change. Elliott said, "You might sell enough birds to buy a whole raft of rafts, Number Three. Let's take a look at that contract."

The damned contract was six pages long and the print was so small that I couldn't of read it even if I had my bifocal fishing glasses on.

"I'm glad you hired a lawyer," said Elliott. "He's the guy to read this. And I'll give you some good advice, Number Three:

"A MAN NEVER NEEDS A LAWYER MORE THAN WHEN HE IS HANDED A 'STANDARD' CONTRACT."

Well, I have included that advice, even though it won't help anyone catch more trout, because Elliott gave me the idea to write these articles in the first place. I figure I owe it to him to share some of his words of wisdom. He doesn't know enough about fishing to advise anybody, but he's a smart man just the same. I'll give George Adams the contract to read, but I have to say I'm not sure he's the man for the job. He was wearing glasses way back in high school so his eyes are no doubt worse 'n mine.

Elliott and I drank the last two beers, then just talked about my upcoming show and how much he was gonna miss it out here and all. Nancy came home and heard all the news. She was real excited about my whittling show, but sad about Elliott leaving. She invited him to stay for dinner but he said he was going out to dinner with Beth. I asked him, then, if Beth knew he was leaving. He said, of course she did. He said they had talked about it all the way home from the Milhous River. I guess there was more talking done that day than there was fish caught. It's funny how that happens.

After Elliott left Nancy hugged me and said she was proud of me, and that she was sorry I was losing my best friend. I told her I wasn't—that she was my best friend. And judging by what happened next (which is none of your business and not meant for the pages of a fishing journal), that was just the right thing to say.

Dear Piscatorial Partners,

I guess I am going to New York with my birds because my lawyer said the contract looked to be "a good straightforward business document." I signed it and he stamped it as a notary for an additional two dollars, which I told him is maybe the slickest racket in America. George had no answer to that but only said, "Now, on to the other contract."

I had almost forgotten about the other contract but he reminded me that it was the one Beth had drawn up. I said I didn't even know she'd finished it, but he said, "Oh yes, she delivered it very promptly. The woman does very professional work," he added. Right off, I wasn't sure whose side he was on.

I was right to worry, too, because he was a whole lot more excited about this contract than he was about the bird deal. He kept saying, "Look at this—more than fair, more than fair," until I began to think it was Beth paying him instead of me. One time he even said, "It's your decision, but I have to say I think you'd be a fool to pass up this business opportunity."

Well, I don't think George Adams would know a fool if he was right across the table from one. I told him I would sit on that one for a while. You know me by now, so you know I meant that it will be a cold day in hell before I sign it. But you just can't be that honest with lawyers or they will get offended. I left his office, mailed the contract to New York, and headed for the Muddler. My month of being thrown out was over and nothing makes you thirstier than arguing with lawyers.

Murphy was awful glad to see me. "It's been terrible boring in here without you, Donnie. Hardly even a broken glass."

I drank two beers real quick, cause Pabst just tastes better in the Muddler than it does at home. Then I slowed down and sipped the third one. I was kinda looking over my shoulder towards the door, hoping Hank would come in so I could pay him back. Murph must of noticed—sometimes a good bartender is almost psychotic, they are so good at reading people's minds. "Relax, Donnie," he said, "that little S.O.B. won't be in. He was bragging so loud about busting you in the nose I threw him out for two months. I don't like him anyway."

I did relax. And I told Murph all about the crazy guy in the museum who was paying my way to New York City. Murph was some impressed.

He said, "Well, I'll be damned. It is hard to picture you in the Big Apple. I hope you're bringing your wife along to keep you out of trouble."

"Of course I'm not," I told him. "New York City is no place for a woman."

Murph just shook his head like he does and went down the bar to wait on his regulars. I drank up and headed for home.

I should of stayed at the Muddler. When I got home

Nancy was reading the mail, and she was so excited I was afraid she would pee her pants. She had a letter in her hands from your editor, Sydney. Tell me the truth: Is Sydney related to Beth in any way? I ask that because they seem to be in cahoots about this bed-and-breakfast deal. Sydney told Nancy that, since it looked like I was going to New York with my "carvings," the women in your club thought it would be great to meet Nancy and hear about "the new bed-and-breakfast fishing lodge we were building."

I guess a lot of 'em think they are coming out here. Obviously they haven't asked their husbands yet. Sydney even suggested a name—The Feminine Line—and told Nancy that she knew two women guides who would be interested in working for us. Sydney said the club would pay Nancy's airfare to New York.

Nancy was almost jumping up and down. She said, "We're going, aren't we, honey?" And when I didn't say anything she looked at me real hard. "You are going to sign the contract, aren't you? Beth showed it to me. Don't you think it's more than fair?"

I didn't answer right away. More than fair is definitely in the eyes of the beholder. I can tell you that. I still didn't think I wanted anything to do with this bed-and-breakfast idea. I sure as hell didn't want to be responsible for no New York women who fancied themselves guides drowning in our dangerous Montana rivers. But when a man's wife is jumping up and down with excitement, and that man's whole life is spent trying to protect her and make her happy, and that man has had three Pabst Blue Ribbons at the Muddler, it is hard to say no. "I already signed it," I said.

That wasn't really a lie. I had signed one contract, but I guess I knew which contract we were talking about. So when Nance ran to call Beth and tell her the "great news," I hollered that I was going to the Muddler. Instead I went and interrupted George Adams's dinner and signed Beth's contract. Now my life is ruined.

But, Say La V! That's what I always say when my life is destroyed. Say La V is a French word meaning "look on the bright side, even if the sun is just a little slash of light hiding behind thunderclouds." I have some French in my bloodstream so it's okay for me to say Say La V. The bright side of this bed-and-breakfast deal is that I will, no doubt, finally be the Number One guide again.

Dear Piscatorial Partners,

It is hard to say "Say La V" when you wake up to the noise of bulldozers on your own property.

It's not a natural sound, I can tell you that. I got my pants on and went outside just in time to see one of my two tamaracks fall over. My dad planted those trees. A five-foot slab broke off when the tree hit the ground. I walked over to it, with the guy on the bulldozer yelling at me, and I dragged it over to my shop. I guess one of these days I'll whittle a sandhill crane out of it.

I looked up to see Nancy standing in the doorway. She was still in her robe and I could swear she was crying. That didn't make any sense at all, because she had just told me last night that this was gonna be the happiest day in her life. I thought about going up and asking her what the hell was wrong, but instead I just gave her a little wave and got in my truck. I needed to get out of there.

It's October twenty-first. Elliott has been gone for almost two months now, and Beth is back in Vermont until sometime in January. The big-game season will open in a couple of days, which means the fishing season is about over. I guess this will be my last letter until next year.

I imagine you New Yorkers aren't much interested in elk hunting, since there are no elk in your neighborhoods. The truth is I'm not much interested myself. I drove around some back roads for a while, making believe I was scouting for elk. But I didn't see none so, after an hour or so, I drove into town and had some breakfast at Trudy's. Then I had a beer at the Muddler. By ten-thirty A.M. I was back home.

Nancy had gone to work but she left me a note. It just said, "I love you, babe." I crumpled it up and threw it in the garbage. I don't know what was wrong with me. Maybe I was trying to catch the flu or something. Anyway, I picked it back up, smoothed it out, and put it in my pocket. Next, I stood looking in the refrigerator for a few minutes, even though I wasn't hungry. Then I went out to my shop. The bulldozers were still working; they were so loud it was hard to concentrate on my whittling. I cut my left hand right away, so I quit. And I guess I should give you one last rule:

IF YOU DRAW BLOOD IN THE FIRST FIVE MINUTES, YOU ARE ENGAGED IN THE WRONG ACTIVITY FOR THAT PARTICULAR DAY.

I don't know if I've ever felt so restless. I looked out at those bulldozers again but I kept seeing my daddy's face and I just couldn't stand it. Finally I went and got Dad's old Leonard fly rod and the new waders Beth and Nancy had bought me to celebrate signing the contract and I headed out to my place. Maybe that would be just what the doctor ordered.

There was a car parked at the trailhead. I guess I wasn't even surprised. Some days are just meant to be that way. I was dumbfounded, though, by the plates. This car wasn't from Montana or even Washington. It was from Illinois. Awful late for tourists; I guess those guys from Chicago never work.

I almost turned around and went home, but all I could think of was bulldozers. So I put on my waders and grabbed the old Leonard. I didn't even take it out of the case, though. Just carried it in the tube, and I didn't hurry down the trail. I just walked. I knew somebody else was already there, and I kept telling myself it didn't matter.

I kept to the trail all the way to the river, didn't bother to go up to the cliff to have a look around. I sure as hell wasn't going to see a bear. The guy was fishing nymphs just below the surface—probably a little bead-head—just what I would of been doing if he hadn't of got there first. I sat down on this big flat rock and opened a Pabst Blue Ribbon. You are probably wondering why I didn't just heave a big rock into this guy's water and head for home. I don't know why myself, except that I guess sitting there, watching another guy fish, beat watching some clown in a bulldozer knock down my father's trees. I wasn't really enjoying myself, though. The guy wasn't catching a damned thing and it irked me to think how well I would no doubt be doing in his place. I was hearing bulldozers every time I looked at the guy. Our ears are always playing tricks on us because they are located even closer to our brains than our eyes are. At first when I started hearing the bulldozers I began gathering a little pile of good throwing rocks without really thinking about it. But I quit that and just decided not to look at the guy. That was getting easier all the time because he was working his way upstream way too fast to really catch fish. I just focused my eyes on the river in front of me and tried not to think of Beth or bed-and-breakfasts or bulldozers. My ears followed my eyes and soon they were just hearing the river, too.

Now, most writers who consider themselves to be experts on fishing fall all over themselves talking for page after page about "reading water." That's all well and good but I say listening is better than reading any day. I made it through high school without reading hardly anything because I listened when the teachers were talking about the books we were supposed to read, and especially when Vicki Purcell, the class brain, read her book reports to the class. I didn't get straight As or even crooked ones but I got by, and I caught a lot more fish than Vicki Purcell did. I'll guaran-damn-tee you that. So I guess you should get your notebook out one more time.

LISTEN TO RIVERS.

You'll be glad you did, even if you can read water, and you probably won't have to buy near as many fishing books, and maybe not half so many of those so-called "self-help" books neither.

I was listening real good. I found myself taking that old Leonard out of the tube and out of its cloth case. I had it all together and a line strung on it before I even remembered that there was already a guy fishing the run. I caught myself in time, though, and looked upstream at that guy from Illinois. He looked like he had forgot all about me. He was fishing even faster than before and his casting had gone all to hell. I guessed that he was like Mr. Hawaii and a lot of other guys us guides have to put up with. He no doubt expected to catch a fish on every cast just because he had spent a passel of money to get to Montana. He didn't make me hear bulldozers anymore. I almost laughed out loud just looking at him, being tickled to death he wasn't my client. But it was more fun looking at and listening to the river; I quit paying any attention at all to Mr. Illinois.

I noticed that the river was sending me a new sound, the quiet slurp of trout rising to feed on the surface. I may need reading glasses, now, but my ears have hardly aged a bit and I can hear trout feeding from even farther than I can cast. Before I gave much thought to what I was doing, I was wading out into the river towards this pod of rising fish.

You folks in the city who are used to reading lies from New Zealand may not really believe that fish rise to dry flies in mid-October so I should stop right here and tell you what kind of day this was. It was afternoon by now and the sun was shining through the trees so warm it was a relief to get up off that rock and wade into the water. The water was cold all right, because we'd already had several good frosts, but we were in the middle now of that late-October warm spell we call our Indian summer. I have no idea why we call it that unless it's because the Indians are still here after all the tourists run for home at the first frost, so they get to enjoy it. I'm sure they don't mind having this sunny season named after them. If they do they can just call it Donnie Phillips's summer, because it's my favorite time of year. It is often sunny and warm and all the tourists are gone, except this impatient ass from Illinois who was trespassing on my water. I turned around when I was only knee deep in the river and saw that he had given up and was heading up the trail toward his rig. Finally, I had the place to myself. I concentrated on the rising fish.

There were five or six fish working within easy casting range, right on the outside lip of the current. Of course I started looking to see what they were eating. It didn't take long. I am a pro, after all. These trout were obviously feeding on a small olive-bodied mayfly. Now, don't start jumping up and down thinking you finally caught ol' Donnie in a lie, because I just told you it's late October and now I'm telling you I was looking at mayflies. Mayflies hatch near year-round in Montana, leastwise when it's warm. They are not so named because they only come around in May. The name "mayfly" is short for "may I fly." These bugs' wings stand straight up from their backs when they float down the river. The upright wings are like a young boy's hands, clasped together over his dinner plate, all ten fingers aimed straight at heaven, waiting for his father to say "amen," so the boy can say, "May I please have some fried chicken."

Mayflies don't eat chicken. They are no doubt saying, "May my wings dry soon so I can fly," or, "May I please float by this pod of feeding fish without being seen."

This particular batch of mayflies I was watching were very small—probably a size eighteen—so their wings didn't reach very far towards heaven, and they weren't having much luck in the prayers-being-answered department. The fish, though, were having a good day, and it was beginning to look like I would, too.

I have lots of mayflies in various sizes, but when I opened my fly box the first fly I spotted was a number sixteen Royal Wulff. That got me thinking about Elliott and Beth and the bed-and-breakfast and New York City, and for a minute I was hearing bulldozers again. It dawned on me that Elliott was no doubt waking up to the noise of bulldozers right inside his house. At least I was only losing trees.

Anyway, for reasons I may never understand, I tied on that strawberry shortcake fly even though the obvious choice was the number eighteen Olive Parachute Mayfly sitting right next to it in my fly box. I dropped my first cast about ten feet above what looked to be the largest of those feeding trout, and it floated right down the feeding lane. He took it with one of those soft rises that just nuzzles the surface of the water.

I set the hook and that old Leonard bent hard against the weight of a heavy fish. Some fish you just know you'll always remember. This one, a big brown, didn't make no showy acrobatic jumps like a rainbow might. He just bulled down in that current and shook his head, trying to break that old Leonard or make me lose patience. That rod and I both did our job, though. The trout made three strong runs away from me, but the fourth time in he was tired. I slid him up on the bank right near the rock I had been sitting on.

He was a beautiful fish, deep bodied and brightly colored with the large hooked jaw of a spawning male. By the time I unhooked him, revived him a bit in the water, and watched him swim away, the other fish in the pod were working again.

But I surprised myself. I sat back down on the rock, took my clippers out of my vest pocket, and clipped that Royal Wulff off my leader. This day, one fish seemed to be enough. I took off my hat and hooked that fly right above the E in BARBLESS "Good luck, Elliott," I said. Then I looked around; I'm not used to talking to myself right out loud. There was no one else around. The river was the only one listening. I said it again, even louder: "Good luck!"